Praise for *New York Times* bestselling author
CHRISTINE WARREN

BLACK MAGIC WOMAN
"Excitement, passion, mystery, characters who thoroughly captivate, and a satisfying romance make [it] a must-read."　　　　　　—*Romance Reviews Today*

"Will capture your senses and ensnare your imagination. Another great novel from Christine Warren."　　　　　　—*Single Titles*

"Sexy, action-packed romance!"—*Joyfully Reviewed*

PRINCE CHARMING DOESN'T LIVE HERE
"Christine Warren's The Others novels are known for their humorous twists and turns of other-worldly creatures. Like her other Others novels, *Prince Charming Doesn't Live Here* is an excellently delicious story with great characterization."
　　　　　　—*Fresh Fiction*

BORN TO BE WILD
"Warren packs in lots of action and sexy sizzle."
　　　　　　—*Romantic Times BOOKreviews*

"Incredible."　　　　　　—*All About Romance*

"Warren takes readers for a wild ride."
　　　　　　—*Night Owl Romance*

"Another good addition to The Others series."
　　　　　　—*Romance Junkies*

"[A] sexy, engaging world . . . will leave you begging for more!"
—*New York Times* bestselling author Cheyenne McCray

BIG BAD WOLF
"In this world . . . there's no shortage of sexy sizzle."
—*Romantic Times BOOKreviews*

"Another hot and spicy novel from a master of paranormal romance." —*Night Owl Romance*

"Ms. Warren gives readers action and danger around each turn, sizzling romance, and humor to lighten each scene. *Big Bad Wolf* is a must-read."
—*Darque Reviews*

YOU'RE SO VEIN
"Filled with supernatural danger, excitement, and sarcastic humor." —*Darque Reviews*

"Five stars. This is an exciting, sexy book."
—*Affaire de Coeur*

"The sparks do fly!" —*Romantic Times BOOKreviews*

ONE BITE WITH A STRANGER
"Christine Warren has masterfully pulled together vampires, shape shifters, demons, and many 'Others' to create a tantalizing world of dark fantasies come to life. Way to go, Warren!"
—*Night Owl Romance*

"A sinful treat."   —*Romance Junkies*

"Hot fun and great sizzle."
                          —*Romantic Times BOOKreviews*

"A hot, hot novel."   —*A Romance Review*

WALK ON THE WILD SIDE
"A seductive tale with strong chemistry, roiling emotions, steamy romance, and supernatural action. The fast-moving plot in *Walk on the Wild Side* will keep the readers' attention riveted through every page, and have them eagerly watching for the next installment."   —*Darque Reviews*

HOWL AT THE MOON
"*Howl at the Moon* will tug at a wide range of emotions from beginning to end . . . Engaging banter, a strong emotional connection, and steamy love scenes. This talented author delivers real emotion which results in delightful interactions . . . and the realistic dialogue is stimulating. Christine Warren knows how to write a winner!"   —*Romance Junkies*

THE DEMON YOU KNOW
"Explodes with sexy, devilish fun, exploring the further adventures of The Others. With a number of the gang from previous books back, there's an immediate familiarity about this world that makes it easy to dive right into. Warren's storytelling style makes these books remarkably entertaining."
                     —*Romantic Times BOOKreviews* (4½ stars)

Also by
Christine Warren

On the Prowl
Not Your Ordinary Faerie Tale
Black Magic Woman
Prince Charming Doesn't Live Here
Born to Be Wild
Big Bad Wolf
You're So Vein
One Bite with a Stranger
Walk on the Wild Side
Howl at the Moon
The Demon You Know
She's No Faerie Princess
Wolf at the Door

Anthologies

The Huntress
No Rest for the Witches

DRIVE ME WILD

Christine Warren

St. Martin's Paperbacks

DRIVE ME WILD

Copyright © 2012 by Christine Warren.

All rights reserved.

For information address St. Martin's Press, 175 Fifth Avenue, New York, NY 10010.

ISBN: 978-0-312-35724-5

Printed in the United States of America

St. Martin's Paperbacks edition / December 2012

St. Martin's Paperbacks are published by St. Martin's Press, 175 Fifth Avenue, New York, NY 10010.

10 9 8 7 6 5 4 3 2 1

To the best friend a girl could have, and not just because you totally got the "here, kitty, kitty" thing.

One

The minute Rafael De Santos stepped out the front door of Vircolac, he knew he was being followed. He could have credited a sort of preternatural sixth sense for the knowledge, a combination of the heightened hearing and sight of his Feline heritage, but that wouldn't have been precisely true. Because the fact was, whoever was tailing him was doing a piss-poor job.

Maybe Rafe's perceptions of this sort of thing had been colored by all the time he'd spent with the Lupines of the Silverback Clan, who were renowned for their abilities at covert actions like tails and stake-outs. It could be that the contrast between their expert maneuvers and the bungling of the figure behind him tonight made an otherwise perfectly adequate tail look inept. Then the tail tripped over a crack in the sidewalk and fell sideways into a garbage can, and Rafe shook his head. No, his stalker really was that bad.

Which begged the question: Why was someone tailing him in the first place? To begin with, Rafe was not in the sort of neighborhood where one was likely to be mugged. Admittedly, crime in Manhattan knew no real borders, but this swanky neighborhood in the Upper East Side was as safe as you were likely to get without abandoning the city entirely. So, he didn't think the tail was a common street thug.

He supposed it could be another Felix come to challenge him for his territory, but judging by the figure's general size and shape—not to mention apparent clumsiness—the upstart would be in for a rude surprise if he attempted anything of the sort. Again, not very likely.

He briefly considered the possibility that it might be another rogue Fae. After the incident a few months ago with Seoc and Fergus and Lucifer and the ruckus caused here and in Faerie by that delegation, just the thought made Rafe nervous. But again, this tail was way too clumsy to be one of the Beautiful People.

So what was left? Rogue Lupine sounded about as likely as a Felix challenger, given their proximity to Graham Winters's home and business. Any werewolf who attempted to act without Graham's consent in the heart of that Alpha's own territory would be three steps past stupid and not a little foolhardy. Such an idiot would likely have charged him by now.

This was a puzzle, and Rafe was enough a man of his blood to be very curious about puzzles.

Keeping his gaze straight ahead and his pace steady, he quietly turned the tables on his stalker and let the hunter become the hunted.

It didn't take much for Rafe to win the upper

hand. In his tailored suit and Italian loafers, he had the advantage of surprise. No one ever expected an obviously wealthy man to know the first thing about defending himself or about tracking prey. Luckily, Rafe was more than just another wealthy man.

He was Felix.

He felt his mouth curve at the inherent arrogance in that statement of fact. There didn't seem to be a way to state it without arrogance. His people had been worshipped as gods centuries before humans ever entertained the thought that a single god might sustain the complexity of life. That sort of thing tended to breed arrogance in a man. Then of course, the very nature of the cat beast within him meant arrogance was indelibly stamped on his nature. The jaguar occupied the top of the food chain in its native jungles of South America. When one had no rivals at all, one stopped seeing rivals even where they existed.

Rafe liked to think of himself as more than just his beast, more than the jaguar spirit that crouched within him. He embraced and appreciated that part of his ancestry, that aspect of his nature, but as a modern civilized man, he liked to think of his nature as more complex than "man by day, jaguar by night."

He had, after all, grown up in a penthouse apartment in Manhattan, not in the dense, tropical jungles of his father's childhood. He had attended private schools and a prestigious university, learned how to ace an exam and order fine wine for sophisticated companions. He knew which fork to use at even the most exalted tables and could debate with intelligence and gusto topics ranging from Kierkegaard to Handel to the politics of Eastern European nationalism. And he could do it all with a droll wit and an urbane smile.

None of that negated the feral predator lurking in his soul. The one that knew it could turn on his would-be stalker and rip out the man's throat before his enemy could even voice a scream in protest. It was the same beast that first realized his stalker smelled like a woman. And not just any woman. She smelled like a witch.

The fragrance roused his curiosity even higher. Witches and werefolk rarely had contact with each other, and it had been that way for as long as Rafe could remember. He had heard a few stories over the years about why that was the case—tales that ranged from ancient race wars inspired by divine edict to a magical version of the Hatfields, the McCoys, and that infamous pig. Rafe doubted either story could claim the crown as the whole truth, but he realized he'd never before bothered to wonder about it. Not until he found himself being stalked by a female witch on a deserted street in Upper Manhattan on a Wednesday night.

Funny how that sort of thing could spring itself on a man.

More determined than ever to satisfy his curiosity and find out what the stalking witch wanted with him, Rafe continued to lead his unsuspecting hunter straight into a trap. He imagined things could get interesting tonight, and after a run of boring business meetings, the diversion might prove to be just what he needed.

Heeere, kitty-kitty-kitty . . .

The singsong call echoed through her head, making Tess Menzies bite down on her lip to stifle a snicker. You wouldn't think her current position—crouched in the shadows of an old brownstone, her eyes glued to the elegant facade of the building across the street—would be one conducive to humor, but then again Tess had always been one to laugh at inappropriate moments. Like when her grandfather was berating her for wearing the wrong outfit to his sixtieth birthday party. He didn't seem to find the humor in telling a fourteen-year-old that her heels were too low and her hemline too long. He hadn't appreciated the joke.

At all.

He probably wouldn't appreciate her fanciful idea about cajoling the most powerful werecat in Manhattan to her side with a ditty and a saucer of milk, either. The man seriously lacked a sense of humor.

Her own sense of humor was what had kept Tess sane for the duration of the most boring night of her life. She'd been lurking at the mouth of this alley for close to three hours, and her muscles had long ago given up their protests over her cramped position. She hoped that wouldn't pose a problem when she tried to

force them to move again. According to the intelligence provided by her grandfather's sources, her
mark should be making his move any second now.

The thought inspired yet more snickering. This
whole episode just screamed for the use of language
like *mark* and *intelligence,* even though the closest
Tess herself had ever come to espionage or intrigue
was watching old Humphrey Bogart movies on satellite. The idea that she'd gone straight from curling
up on her sofa in Tribeca on dateless Saturday nights
with a bowl of popcorn and the opening credits of
The Maltese Falcon to staking out a private club on
the Upper East Side . . .

Well, the comic implications of that just went on
forever.

She supposed her grandfather could have picked
someone less suitable for carrying out this particular
favor, but she figured it would have taken a lot of time
and some serious effort. After all, she knew of one
former marine, three former police officers, a retired
private investigator, and a (mostly) reformed thief just
in her grandfather's immediate circle of friends. Any
of them could probably have located this particular
shapeshifter and delivered the council's message with
a tenth of the fuss and muss Tess instinctively knew
she would cause given half the chance. Not to brag,
but she had a knack for that kind of thing—namely,
for turning a simple task into something out of an
Abbott and Costello movie.

What could she say? It was a gift.

You'd think her grandfather would take that into consideration before giving her this assignment. But no. When Grandfather got a notion into his head, nothing short of a seismic catastrophe could shake him from his course, and the jury still deliberated over whether even that could do the job.

Sighing, Tess wrapped her arms around herself and chafed her hands up and down to try to generate some heat. The crisp October night that had felt so pleasant just an hour ago had taken a decidedly chilly turn. She indulged in a moment of regret that she hadn't stopped to fill a thermos with coffee before she set herself up here to wait, but shrugged it off. If she had coffee, she'd be drinking it, and if she drank coffee, she'd have to pee, so it really was just as well. She couldn't exactly knock on the door of the building she was using for concealment and ask to use their bathroom. She'd probably give the poor owners a heart attack, and wouldn't that justify her grandfather's opinion of her?

Since she recalled once having read somewhere that the best cure for boredom on a stakeout was fantasizing, Tess let her mind wander down that path for a minute. She could just picture herself clad head-to-toe in black, from her black jeans and supple black boots to her thin black turtleneck sweater. She looked more like a cat burglar than anything else. Not exactly a reassuring sight to find on one's doorstep at two thirty-seven AM.

She swallowed another chuckle and shifted her

weight subtly, her gaze still on the doors across the street. Her little fantasy was probably way off base, though. Judging by the ornately carved doors of the buildings around her, the beautiful historical architecture, and the pricey addresses, no one on this block or the next answered his own door, even at two thirty-seven AM. That, she assumed with a smirk, was what butlers were for.

In that respect, Tess was certainly out of her element here in the land of milk and money. Her own perfectly adequate loft a block shy of SoHo would probably fit inside the foyers of most of the houses on this street, especially the house she currently had her eye on. The four-story limestone building sat in the middle of the block like a grande dame holding court. No signage marred the exquisite facade—unless you counted the classic brass address numbers as a sign— nor did any other marks indicate that Tess had staked out one of the most exclusive and prestigious private clubs in all of Manhattan.

But then, when your club catered to vampires, werewolves, and other creatures of the night, neon was probably not a particularly discreet choice.

For at least the last two centuries, Vircolac had easily retained its title as the best-kept secret in Manhattan. The only reason Tess had learned of it was because the Witches' Council had a vested interest in some of the people who passed through its thick, oak doors.

Well, *people* might not exactly be the correct term,

since the membership of Vircolac consisted entirely of the less human members of New York society. Vampires, werewolves, and shapeshifters of all kinds filled the club's membership list, and the only humans who ever made it past the doorman were rumored to be closely connected with the club's owner, Graham Winters. A werewolf himself, Winters ran the club like a medieval kingdom, and unless the general consensus had things entirely wrong, Vircolac generated about as much income as the average kingdom. Most people referred to it as a business empire, and for a single club to gain that distinction meant that Graham Winters probably had more money pass through his fingers on a daily basis than Tess's little herb shop in the East Village could expect to generate between now and the end of time.

It must be good to be the king.

In addition to his duties to his business, Winters supposedly kept an equally tight rein on the Silverback Clan, the werewolf pack he led and the single largest collection of shapeshifters in Greater Manhattan. As Alpha, he was directly responsible for every single member of that pack, and he was said to take the job very seriously.

In his spare time, Tess supposed wryly.

Winters, though, was not why she was crouching in the shadows of some garbage bins on a Wednesday night in October. She didn't have to deal with the werewolf, thank the gods. Instead, her grandfather had sent her here to bell the cat.

Rolling her eyes, Tess shifted her weight and sighed.

Right. Like she was so qualified to chase down a werecat with nothing more going for her than a diplomatic message and a sunny disposition. Blond hair, blue eyes, and a curvy figure against 350 pounds of muscle, razor-sharp teeth, and claws like tiny, lethal daggers? Sure, those were great odds.

Looking back at her conversation with her grandfather, Tess could recall bringing up those very salient points to him just yesterday. She had mentioned that she was absolutely the worst person for the job of delivering an official message from the council. Heck, she wasn't even a *member* of the Witches' Council, let alone a representative. She had precisely no knowledge of nor experience with werefolk of any kind (not that many witches did, since the two groups tended to avoid each other like a particularly nasty strain of the Ebola virus), and generally Tess tended to end up with her foot in her mouth at any and all available opportunities. So what made her the choice for this assignment again?

Oh, right. Grandfather's standard answer. "Because I said so."

Tess grumbled to herself and pressed the button on the side of her watch to illuminate the dial. According to the information the council had provided, the werecat she'd come to see was already ten minutes later than his regular timetable indicated. Apparently he didn't realize he had a stalker with better things to do with her time. Sighing, she trained her gaze back on the door to Vircolac and settled in for an extended wait.

She didn't get one.

Almost as soon as she had the carved oak doors back in her sight, the right side opened and a figure stepped out. It paused for a moment to speak to someone on the threshold.

"Finally," she breathed, freezing in place, gaze fastened on the man across the street.

She got a brief look at his face while he stood in the pool of light cast by the fixture over the club's doors, so she knew this was her guy. His features had the angular, slightly exotic cast of his Latin ancestors, and even in the artificial light she saw the bronze hue of his skin and the way his black hair gave off almost blue highlights. Add to that the tailored fit of his suit, the arrogant, graceful way he held himself, and the liquid quality to the way he moved, and Tess had no doubts. She had a bead on Rafael De Santos.

The problem was that she hadn't expected him to be quite so mouthwateringly gorgeous.

Tess sat mesmerized for several minutes before a moth flying perilously close to her cheek reminded her that not only was her mouth gaping open like the legs of a cheerleader on prom night, her tongue was probably hanging out, too. She clamped her jaw shut with a click, but her reaction seemed almost beyond her control.

The man took her breath away.

For some reason she'd had this picture in her head of the shapeshifter as unappealing, sort of bestial and feral, his humanity a thin veil over his more savage nature. She knew that image didn't exactly mesh with his reputation as a charming if feckless rogue, more Casanova than killer, but her mind had discounted the stories as rumor. No one could be as handsome and charming as the stories made out, not unless he worked in Hollywood and regularly appeared on the covers of national magazines.

But now here Tess was, finding them to be absolute fact. If not shameful understatements.

The only evidence she saw of this man's bestial side was the animal magnetism she could feel rolling off him, even from fifty feet away. It made her fingers itch, her mouth dry out, and her—

Well, she really didn't want to think about what her other parts were doing.

Focus, Tess. Focus.

Dragging her eyes off the werecat's butt— conveniently positioned toward her as he spoke with the figure in the doorway—Tess ordered her heart to slow down and her thighs to unclench so she could get back to the task at hand. She'd need all her faculties operational for this one. She could just feel it.

Why does he have to be so gorgeous?

She eased herself to her feet and hugged the side of the stairway, completely engulfed in the shadows. She would be a lot more relaxed about taking a message to the leader of the Council of Others if he were a short, ugly were-gopher instead of a take-me-now jungle beast of a heartthrob.

Where's the justice in the universe? she silently cried.

No one answered.

Great. Now even my own subconscious is ignoring me.

She waited for him to wave farewell to the doorman and start off down the deserted street before easing from her hiding place and trailing after him in the shadows. She made it approximately three steps before she tripped over her own feet and went stumbling sideways into a trash can. Thankfully, it was plastic and not the old-fashioned metal kind. With that much noise, she might as well just have shouted his name.

She felt kind of stupid following him like this— instead of walking right up to him, introducing herself, and taking care of business like a reasonable adult—but not stupid enough to change her approach. She told herself she was taking a few minutes to build up her courage before taking the plunge. She just wished she were naive enough to believe it.

She would have to speak to him eventually, of course. It would be difficult to deliver the message otherwise. What she needed was an appropriate ice breaker.

Okay, so how about, *Excuse me, Mr. De Santos? I have some information you might be interested in.*

No. Too Jehovah's Witness.

Um . . . *Hey, are you Rafael De Santos, the famous werejaguar and leader of the Council of Others?*

Nope. Too Bellevue escapee.

Mr. De Santos, I come bearing an urgent message from the High Authority of the Witches' Council.

Ugh! Too sci-fi B movie.

Hm, maybe, *Mr. De Santos, my name is Tess Menzies, and I'm—oof!*

The "oof!" was never intended to be part of the speech, but it's what burst out of her mouth when two hundred and some-odd pounds of male muscle barreled into her from the side and drove her deep into a service alley halfway down the street.

Before she had time to yell *Fire!*—and she called herself a native New Yorker—she was pressed flat against the brick wall of one of the adjacent buildings with her hands yanked over her head and six feet of man pinning her in place.

"Who are you, and why the hell have you been following me?"

His growl rumbled through her with a menace she could feel down in her bones, and she knew instinctively that if he'd given her a full-fledged roar, she'd be fighting for control of her bladder right about now. Even so, his efforts would probably have made a normal person cry. The man had intimidation down to an art. He projected pure rage and menace, and the snarl he rumbled out right up against her face did manage to make her take a hearty gulp, but she rallied quickly and dealt with the situation the way she always did: She brazened through it.

"Sheesh." She managed to get it out without squeaking and congratulated herself. "If you usually come on to women this strongly, I have to wonder that you ever get a date."

What the hell are you doing? a voice inside her demanded.

I have absolutely no idea, she answered.

He snarled again. Lower this time. More menacing. "I said, who the hell are you?"

"I heard you." She swallowed a knot of fear and lifted her chin. "I just didn't think it was any of your business."

His expression, which she could see clearly, given its current location about a nanometer away from hers—he had really great skin, she noticed, all smooth and even and bronze—turned incredulous.

"Pardon me? Unless I'm very much mistaken— and I know I'm not—you've been tailing me for three blocks. That makes your name, rank, serial number, and intentions very much my business."

She forced a carefree grin and watched his golden eyes blaze. She hoped he wouldn't notice the panic lurking in hers.

"Well, my name is Tess, my rank is absolutely nothing, I'm horrible with numbers, and my intentions are a little too complicated to explain to you in a dark alley. Plus, I generally talk with my hands, and you're currently making that a wee bit difficult."

He snarled. "I have no time for smart-aleck re-torts. Why are you following me?"

She blinked up at him with wide blue eyes that generally made men smile at her indulgently while telling her to let them handle things and not worry her pretty little head. "Well, I thought that would be obvious. I wanted to know where you were going."

He was ignoring the eyes.

How could he ignore the eyes?

"Not good enough. Explain. Now."

Tess blinked, her mouth curving into the standard plan B pout. "That's the truth. I wanted to know where you were going. You know, for someone with such a reputation for being a ladies' man, you could use a little work on your manners."

"My manners are fine when I'm with a lady. I'm not entirely sure you qualify."

"Hey! What's that supposed to mean?"

"It means that in my experience, ladies don't fol-low men through deserted streets at two thirty in the morning. That's what criminals and cowards do."

The pout had clearly failed as miserably as the big blue eyes, and suddenly Tess felt a lot less confi-dent about her plan C. It didn't seem to be working. At all. Instead of simultaneously being smitten with her 1940s pin-up girl looks and completely underes-timating both her intelligence and her character, the werecat appeared to be pissed off at her. His exotic amber eyes looked hard and impatient, and his sen-sual mouth looked tight and unamused. This was not the sort of reaction she was used to getting from men.

Shifting nervously, she tried tugging her hands free, but his grip only tightened. She gave a hard yank, and he responded with a low warning growl. Before she could seriously give in to panic and start struggling, he leaned into her and used his body to keep her immobile against the cold brick wall.

"Your explanation. Now."

Tess swallowed hard. It was about the only movement she could make. He kept her hands pinned above her head, and now his chest crushed her flat while his hips pressed tightly against hers, rendering her completely immobile. She could feel the way he bent his legs to even out their heights, because those legs crowded against hers to keep her still. She couldn't move a damned muscle, which meant she also couldn't cast any damned spells. She was helpless. Time for plan D: the truth.

Just not too much of it.

"I already explained, sort of. I was supposed to wait for you outside Vircolac until you came out. Then I was supposed to deliver a message and leave. But I got curious to see where you were going in the wee hours of the morning."

She made her tone and expression sullen, as if she had given in reluctantly. Which she had, so that could go in the truth column.

"If you hadn't jumped me, you'd never have known I was following you. I was just going to see if you were going to a nightclub or something. I've never been to one and thought it would be fun to see where the cool ones are. I didn't mean anything by it."

That last part was, perhaps, fodder for the second column.

"What message?"

"Don't ask me. It's written down in a sealed envelope. It's not like I read it or anything."

That one, too.

She saw his nostrils flare as he inhaled deeply. His eyes narrowed. "You're lying. I can smell it on you." He paused, then inhaled again, leaning in a little until Tess's breath caught in her throat. "I can smell something else, too. There's something . . ." Another sniff. ". . . different about you."

Tess felt her eyes widen before she caught herself. "Well, I showered right before I left home," she joked weakly, trying to shift even an inch away from him. "If you can smell me, I think I need to switch soaps."

He didn't appear to be listening. Instead he leaned forward and pressed his face into the curve of her neck. She froze as her stomach clenched. She felt the stir of his breath against her skin and choked on a swift shock of arousal. Apparently, her body hadn't forgotten its first impression of him. It remembered quite clearly how attracted she'd been. And it chose now to remind her.

"That's not it," he muttered, and she could feel the movement of his lips as he spoke. "You smell . . .

different . . ." Sniff. "Exotic . . ." Sniff . . . "Power-ful . . ." Sniff, sniff. Then the dart of a tongue that rasped against her throat. Her knees quivered. "Other."

His head turned, and Tess found herself staring into golden eyes that blazed with impossible heat above a mouth drawn thin in accusation.

"You smell like a witch."

Tess stared up into those amber eyes and felt her first wave of fear. Suddenly she remembered that this man wasn't just a man. He was a Felix—an Alpha werecat—and the most powerful Feline in the history of the city. If he wanted, he could tear out her throat with a swipe of his finger. With the tension radiating off him, she was no longer sure he didn't intend to do just that.

"Well? Are you a witch?" He asked it in that rasping growl and shook her by the hands he held pinned. "You aren't human. I can smell it."

"You smell wrong." She could feel how wide her eyes had grown, but this time it wasn't a ploy. It was fear. "I am human. My name is Tess Menzies."

He pressed his nose against the hollow below her ear and inhaled. She had to bite back a moan as her womb clenched. Never in her life had she reacted to a man like this.

Shit, her timing sucked.

"You're not. Humans smell . . . muddy. Thick. You smell clear. Sweet. Spicy." Again that tongue, rasping like damp sandpaper across her skin. "Taste that way, too. Not human at all."

Fear prodded her into temper. "Eaten many humans, have you?"

She felt his mouth shift into a grin.

"A few here and there." He paused. Nuzzled. Purred softly, "Want me to eat you?"

That sensual, amused question had nothing to do with consumption, but a hell of a lot to do with sex. Sheesh. Did the man usually come on to women when he had them pinned against the wall during an interrogation?

The image brought a flood of moisture between her legs, and she cursed.

"Hmm, smells like you like the idea." A lazy stroke of the tongue. The soft, delicate scrape of teeth. "I'd love to taste that cream I can smell. I bet it's thick and rich and hot."

His legs shifted, forced hers apart. He settled between them until she could feel the ridge of an impressive erection nestling against her mound.

"I'd like to lap it all up. And I will. Just as soon as you answer my question."

"Qu—question?"

Her stammer made him chuckle, and she gritted her teeth.

"Yes, question." He nuzzled the sweet spot below her ear and pressed his hips against hers when she tried to squirm away. "The one where I asked if you're a witch."

If he really wanted to know what she was, *horny*

was the most honest answer she could come up with, but she didn't feel inclined to share that little tidbit.

If she were smart, she wouldn't be sharing any of her tidbits with this man. He was trouble.

"I told you," she gritted out, "my name is Tess, and I'm as human as the next person."

"Considering the next person at the moment is not human at all, that fails to convince me of anything."

This time when she experienced the scrape of his teeth, she could feel the elongated canines, and she squeaked. He didn't sink them into her flesh, and she didn't expect him to, but the message was clear. He was far from human and far from civilized, no matter what he looked like on the surface.

"It's the truth."

He pulled back then and stared down at her with eyes that had gone molten. Even in the darkness, she could see the way his pupils had elongated to feline slits.

"You are very stubborn, and very wrong. Also very unsurprised to find a man with fangs and cat's eyes pinning you up against an alley wall. Would you care to explain why?"

She raised an eyebrow. "Not really."

"Do it anyway."

Stalling for time seemed like her best bet. Well, honestly, it seemed about as hopeless as anything else, but it made her feel better. "How about you let go of my hands first and give me some breathing room? This Spanish Inquisition thing is getting kind of uncomfortable."

"I find it very comfortable indeed," he purred, shifting his hips to press his erection harder against her. "The way you breathe now is positively entrancing, room or no room. But if you truly wish to be free, I suggest you begin to cooperate."

Tess had never taken suggestions very well. "Or what? You'll beat the answers out of me?"

He shifted his grip, transferring both her wrists to one of his large hands, and though she redoubled her efforts, she still couldn't break that grip.

"Hm, would you like that, sweet Tess? Would you like it if I turned you over my knee, bared that lovely bottom to the moonlight, and turned it pink and glowing with the weight of my hand?" His free hand slid around her back and cupped her bottom, kneading the muscle and making her quiver. "Would you like that, *gatita*?"

Christ. Although she'd never been into bondage, the mental image caused an unexpected jolt in her pussy. She ignored it and concentrated on not wrapping her legs around his waist. "Trust a man to resort to violence."

"Only if it pleases you, sweetheart."

"What would please me is you letting me go!"

That damned chuckle again. "Ah, but that would not please me, sweet Tess, and since I am currently the one in control here, it is my wish that counts."

Tess harrumphed. "And isn't that just like a man?"

"Or like a beast." His eyes flashed, and his gaze slid to her lips. "And you know the truth about beasts and beauties, don't you? The beasts always take what they want and damn the consequences."

Her only warning was a flash of gold before his head dipped, and his mouth settled hot and hungry over hers.

Two

Rafe purred his approval at the first taste of her. Rich and sweet, it made him want to lap her up like whipping cream. Her lips parted readily beneath his, probably more from shock than desire, but he pressed his advantage. His tongue slid inside to tease and taste, exploring her flavors and textures like a mapmaker charting new territory. She was more than he had expected, and the power of her threatened to swamp his senses.

He leaned into her, acquainting his body with hers, learning the heat and scent and curve of her. He felt the tension in her muscles and the subtle yielding in her lips as they began to cling to his.

Christ, she tasted good. Her flavor seemed to deepen with each hungry sip, flooding through him and feeding his arousal.

He'd thought at first it was just reflex. When he'd felt himself begin to harden against her hips, he'd written it off as a natural and unavoidable reaction to his proximity to an attractive woman. After all, she'd been pressed up against him like a lover, and he had a healthy sex drive. It was only natural.

What wasn't natural was the way her scent wrapped around him, teasing him with that indefinable foreign quality that had piqued his curiosity. It tickled the edges of his brain like a forgotten memory, an indefinable something that he should recognize, whatever it might be. He felt like he knew what it was if he could just concentrate . . .

Then she whimpered against his mouth, and he felt his curiosity fading. It didn't matter who she was. Didn't matter that her scent was getting stronger as her arousal flared, getting muskier, hotter, smelling more intensely of magic—

The thought slammed the door on his libido.

Magic. Witch. Liar.

He wrenched his mouth away from hers and snarled. "Damn you. Tell me who the hell you are. What kind of witch are you?"

His question startled a laugh out of her, curving those kiss-swollen lips in surprise. "The regular kind, I guess. I didn't know we came in thirty-one flavors."

Damn, but he'd like to taste every flavor she did come in.

He stuffed the thought down and lifted his body away from temptation. "So I was right."

She must have read the skepticism in his face, because she shrugged and scowled. "It's not like I was lying. Just because I'm a witch doesn't mean I'm not human."

He wasn't in the mood to debate her. He'd lived among humans all his life. He knew how they smelled, how they tasted, and he knew she was different.

"So tell me why you were following me. What does a witch want with a shapeshifter in a dark alley in the middle of the night?" Unable to resist, he leaned forward to nuzzle the rapid pulse at the base of her throat. "Aside from the obvious."

"I'm not the one who forced us into the alley, Einstein, so why don't you tell me?"

He felt her struggles, but he also heard the barely audible hitch in her breathing and knew her confrontational facade was an act. "I asked first."

"Oh, and this is suddenly the third grade? Fine. Like I said, I was following you."

He lowered his head to snarl at her and noticed how she licked her lips and jerked away. So his little Tess didn't want his kisses? Or maybe she didn't want to want them. He smiled.

"I knew you were following me, sweet Tess." He bent his head, nuzzled the line of her jaw, flicked his tongue out to taste her skin. "Now I want to know why."

He felt her jaw clench under his tongue. "I already told you, I was supposed to deliver a message, and I got curious."

The hand on her ass shifted, squeezed. "And why would you have any kind of message for me, sweet Tess? You don't even know me, do you?"

She snorted, the sound less than elegant but very clear. "Your name appears in the papers so often, you practically have your own section. I doubt there's a person in Manhattan who doesn't know you."

He digested that as he flicked his tongue against her earlobe. She quivered in his arms. "You may be right. But with all those people who know who I am, very few of them have ever tried tailing me through the streets in the middle of the night. Unless they planned to mug me. Were you planning to mug me?"

"Were you planning to check yourself into Bellevue?"

"I didn't think so." He'd get the truth out of her eventually. Even if he had to keep her here for hours.

He nuzzled her ear, inhaling that intoxicating scent. Days even.

His hand stroked her truly fine ass through a layer of snug denim. No sign of a panty line. Did she wear a thong? Or nothing at all.

Maybe weeks.

"You need to tell me what sort of message you have for me, sweet Tess, before I find something else to occupy myself." He pressed his erection against her belly and felt her freeze.

"Let me go, and I'll tell you."

"Tell me, and I'll let you go."

She gave a credible growl of frustration that made him grin against the curve of her shoulder. "When I get free, I am so turning you into a guppy and feeding you to my neighbor's cat."

"Tell me, Tess, before I decide I don't care about the answer."

She bucked one last time against his hold before falling into a sulk. "I told you, I never saw the damned message. It was given to me in a sealed envelope."

"Tess . . ."

She scowled at him. "That's the truth, damn it. I was told to deliver the message to you, unopened, when you left the Council meeting tonight."

He pulled back to frown down at her. "What Council meeting?"

Tess rolled her eyes. "Just because I was careless enough to let you see me tailing you does not make me terminally stupid. What Council do you think I'm interested in that meets at one AM on the nights of the new moon?"

"And what would an ordinary, very human witch know about the Council of Others?"

Suddenly her luscious scent and feminine body slipped a few notches down on his priority list. At least for the moment. The Council of Others, of which he was the reluctant head, had operated for centuries in the city without incident, mainly because it kept itself a guarded secret from the mortal world. If this woman knew about them, they could have a serious problem on their hands. If she had succeeded in tracing him to the Council chambers in the secret basement at Vircolac, the consequences would be far reaching and bordering on disastrous.

The sobering thought had his hand sliding away from her ass and bracing against the wall beside her head.

"Not a whole hell of a lot, or I wouldn't have had to wait for you outside until it was over, would I? Because everything I could find out about it told me it didn't officially exist." She glared at him from big blue eyes that should have looked innocent, but instead snapped with fire and irritation. "You seem to have better security than the Pentagon."

He dismissed that. "The Pentagon has lousy security. But you knew I was on the Council. You should not even know the Council exists."

"If it's any consolation, I didn't know until two weeks ago."

"And what happened two weeks ago?"

She paused, and he could almost see her weighing her answer. "I got assigned to tail you."

"You have been tailing me for two weeks?" The thought blindsided him. Surely he'd have noticed that kind of presence. He still had instincts. He couldn't have gotten that soft, not even living in the middle of a city for so long. "That is impossible."

She rolled her eyes. "And you're so modest, too. No wonder all the ladies go for you."

He felt his eyes narrow, and he pressed back up against her. "Shall we see how quickly I can make you go for me, sweet Tess? Or would you like to confine your comments to answering my questions?"

Rafe watched her mouth open, then close again with a snap. He waited for a moment before he continued. "Were you watching me for two weeks?"

"Not exactly. I kept track of when you were seen

in public places to get an idea of your schedule, but I wasn't tailing you."

That sounded an awful lot like being tailed to him. "If you kept turning up wherever I was going, I should have noticed you."

Again, she rolled her eyes. It seemed to be a habit. "Right. Like you notice every woman who stares at you when you're going about your business. Garfield, you are so used to being ogled, you don't even see it happening anymore. I would have needed to slip my hand down your pants to get your attention most days. And I'm sure more than one of the other women watching you seriously considered that option."

He found that to be a very distracting mental image. Not the other women, but the idea of this woman, who smelled of spice and magic, sliding her hand down his pants. He imagined the feel of her smooth fingers curving around his shaft, and growled. He apparently needed to keep his thoughts on a leash around this little witch.

"But there was no reason for you to pay attention to me," she continued. "I didn't follow you from place to place, just occasionally popped up where you were, noted the time, and left. I wasn't stupid enough to think you wouldn't have noticed if I had been tailing you."

"All right, I'll set that aside. For the moment." He eyed her pointedly. "I still want to know who hired you and what they want."

"I can't tell you what they want." She must have

seen his mouth open to protest, because she quickly cut him off. "I'm just the messenger. I don't know the text of the message, and I imagine that if they had wanted me to know about it, they wouldn't have given it to me in a sealed envelope. You'll have to read it yourself, and if that's not good enough, I guess you'll just have to go and ask them what they want."

He snarled. "And just who are they?"

She drew a deep breath, blew it out, and glared at him. "The Witches' Council."

The Witches' Council?

Rafe frowned and pulled back another inch. He'd never even heard of a council of witches. Oh, he knew there were witches in the world, and that obviously meant that some of them lived in Manhattan, but he hadn't known they were organized. Of course, as far as he knew, the last diplomatic contact between a witch and the Others in New York had happened in 1627, at the end of a long and protracted dispute over territory and visibility to the humans. Given that fact, Rafe being in the dark about the current magic users' situation wasn't that surprising. Of course, with the distraction presented by the very attractive and very sweet-smelling Tess, he thought that just remembering the whole 1627 thing was pretty damned impressive.

He looked down at said distraction and flexed his hands around her wrists, not so much squeezing as kneading the captive limbs. "So you're a witch who was hired by a Witches' Council to follow me and confront me in a dark alley, but you don't know what they want with me?"

"Like I said, they didn't see fit to share any of the details."

Rafe gave in to temptation long enough to lean in close and taste her skin again. Her fear was fading, making her sweeter, and her irritation increasing, making her hotter. Damn, he could make a meal of her. If his curiosity would leave him in peace.

"Would you care to hazard a guess?"

"What, are we playing twenty questions now?"

He had to stifle the urge to grin at her expression. Somehow the narrowed eyes, twisted lips, and crinkled nose looked less than threatening on her. The curls—dark gold limned in silver in the faint light—and those big blue eyes just spoiled the effect. He schooled his expression into a feral mask and scraped his teeth delicately along her jawline.

"Not yet," he purred, "but we could. I could ask you what you taste like, what you look like spread out on silk sheets, how much it would take to make you beg me to touch you . . ." He lapped at the sensitive skin beneath her chin. "Do you want to play that game with me, sweet Tess?"

He heard the desire as well as the defiance in her snort. "What part of this conversation has been about what I want?"

He chuckled. "Why don't you tell me what you

want, sweet Tess." He paused to inhale deeply, catching the ripeness of her scent. "Or better still, I can tell you what you want . . ."

She shivered in his arms, and the telltale motion made him smile. His little witch was just as affected by him as he was by her. That offered some interesting possibilities.

"I have another idea," she said, and her voice sounded strained. "How about I just give you the bloody message, you let me go, and we both pretend this never happened?"

"Oh, I don't think so, Tess. I think we have much too much to talk about for that to happen. No, I think you should come with me."

He pulled her wrists down in front of her and tugged her away from the wall and toward the street beyond the alley. He managed to move her about seven feet before the surprise wore off and she dug in her heels.

"Wait. Where are we going?"

"To the building I just left. A friend of mine lives there. He'd be happy to provide us with someplace to discuss this message of yours where it's a bit more comfortable. And better lit."

She tugged at her hands and refused to budge. "You're going to take me to Vircolac?"

"So now you know about the club as well?"

"I was waiting for you outside it a few minutes ago, wasn't I?"

"It's not supposed to be common knowledge."

"It isn't. That's why I'm surprised you'd think of taking me there. I thought humans were barred from ever setting foot inside."

He smiled as he remembered Missy Winters's opinion of that particular decree. "The rules have been . . . relaxed a bit recently."

"I don't care. I'm not taking any more chances tonight. If you want to keep talking to me, you can keep talking to me in the alley. I'm perfectly comfortable here."

He turned back to her and raised an eyebrow. "But I am not," he purred. "And unless you intend to make me more comfortable—which, I feel I should warn you, would involve taking off all your clothes and lying down beneath me for three or four hours—I suggest you come with me to the club."

She leaped for the opposite sidewalk with such speed, she almost ended up dragging him along behind her.

In the darkness, Rafe laughed and wondered how long it would take him to change her mind about the appeal of that particular manner of getting comfortable.

Three

"Who is she?"

"Her name is Tess Menzies. I found her lying in wait for me outside the club."

"Outside *my* club? And security didn't see her?"

"They must not have." Rafe shrugged, handed Tess a mug of steaming coffee, and turned away from her as if she didn't exist. She glared at his back. "Maybe they want to be a little more careful in the future."

"Maybe they want to look for new jobs."

The man who growled that threat was none other than Graham Winters himself, the werewolf owner of Vircolac and supposedly one of Rafe De Santos's closest friends. Tess watched the byplay between the two men over the rim of her coffee cup.

"In their defense," Rafe conceded, "it's not like she is just some random human. She is a witch, and apparently one who has been spying on me for several days without me noticing, so we cannot exactly call her easy to spot."

"A witch? What the hell does a witch want with one of us?"

"Damned if I know. She said she had some sort of message to deliver to me. From the Witches' Council."

"They have a council?"

"So she says."

Graham growled something Tess didn't catch, and Rafe laughed.

Scowling, Tess set aside her coffee cup and crossed her arms over her chest. "You know, she also has ears, a mouth, and a fully functional brain. You might want to try talking to me, instead of talking about me as if I weren't even in the room."

Rafe turned to her and raised an eyebrow. "You did not seem so willing to talk to me when we were outside a few minutes ago."

"You had me pinned to the wall like Torquemada with PMS. I was supposed to want to tell you my life story?"

Graham quickly covered a burst of laughter behind a deep cough. Tess and Rafe both turned to glare at him.

"Sorry," the wolf grinned, unrepentant. "Say, what do you think about checking out this note and seeing what all the fuss is about? I mean, it is almost four in the morning, so I'm guessing that whatever it is this Witches' Council wanted to talk to you about, Rafe, it's got to be fairly important, right?"

Rafe growled something that sounded remarkably similar to what Graham had growled about his security people a few minutes ago and stalked back to

Tess's chair. He held out his hand. "Give me the message."

She didn't know how it happened, but all of a sudden she found herself looking from his hand to his face and back again while the devil prodded her tongue to make it do evil things. "Say please."

Graham practically choked to death, but Rafe just closed his eyes, drew a deep breath, and said, "Please," through tightly clenched teeth.

Tess pursed her lips, reached into the pocket of her black denim jacket, and pulled out a slightly crinkled white envelope. She handed it to him with a haughty sniff.

"Thank you," he bit out.

"You're welcome."

Tess watched as he ripped the envelope open and pulled out a single sheet of white paper with her grandfather's seal at the top and the familiar, regimented handwriting marching across the page. She wasn't close enough to read the text, and when Rafe turned away, beginning to pace as he read, she couldn't see the letter at all. But that didn't matter. She already knew what it said.

Not because she'd read the actual text of the letter; she hadn't been lying—about that, at least—but because she had eavesdropped on her grandfather when he and some fellow council members had composed it. Still, she kept quiet while Rafe read.

"They want to meet with the Council," he finally

said, raising his head and handing the letter to Graham. "With me, they say. I am not sure if my name is simply there because I am current head of the Council, or because they have some need to speak with me in particular. Damn Dmitri, anyway."

Graham grinned and shook his head. "Now, now. It's not Misha's fault he has better things to do these days than occupy that Council seat."

"That does not mean I cannot blame him. It makes me feel good to blame him."

Tess watched their conversation with a small frown. She didn't quite know what they were talking about, and she hated feeling left in the dark. "Who are Dmitri and Misha?"

"They're the same person. A friend of ours." Rafe dismissed the question casually and turned to face her, crossing his arms over his chest. "But I think it is still my turn to ask the questions, Tess. Tell me why this council wants to talk to me."

She shrugged, growing wary again. "I don't know. They didn't explain anything to me. They just asked me to deliver the message."

"Yes, and that is what puzzles me at the moment. Why you? If Graham or I were going to deliver a message to someone we did not know and did not trust, but whom we believed might pose a threat to our basic safety, I doubt either of us would choose someone like you to deliver it."

She scowled. "Why not? Because I'm not some

sort of trained spy who would have been able to follow you all the way to the pearly gates without being spotted?"

Rafe shook his head, his lips quirking. "No, because you are small, soft, female, and much too appealing and vulnerable to have been sent to wait outside in the streets of Manhattan alone at three in the morning."

She rolled her eyes. "It wasn't even midnight when I started, and for gods' sakes, I'm a witch. It's not like I'm the world's easiest prey for muggers."

"I didn't seem to have any trouble with you."

"You weren't trying to mug me."

"I should sincerely hope not."

The last comment came from the door of the large study where the three of them had been talking, announcing the arrival of a petite blond woman with big brown eyes and a pretty, gentle face. She wore a long, man's flannel robe with the sleeves rolled up to expose her hands and the hem dragging the floor. Tess thought she saw bunny-shaped slippers peeking out from underneath the plaid fabric as the woman stepped into the room.

She looked from Tess to Rafe to Graham and back to Tess, then smiled a sweet smile that perfectly suited her face and all but radiated kindness. "I'm Missy Winters. I didn't know we had visitors, or I might have stopped to get dressed before seeing what had become of my suspiciously disappearing husband."

Graham crossed the room, a scowl on his face and a blanket he'd grabbed off the back of the comfortable-looking leather sofa in his hands. "You should have gotten dressed anyway." He flicked the blanket open and wrapped it around his wife. "Rafe, close your eyes."

Tess watched while Missy rolled her eyes at her husband and playfully pushed him away. The woman settled next to Tess on the matching leather love seat and offered her the blanket instead.

"Ignore my husband," Missy said. "He's a man, and a Lupine, and the pack Alpha, which means he's slightly insane. I, on the other hand, am female, and human, and therefore very happy to meet you and find out what brings you here at this time of night."

Bemused, Tess found herself smiling back at the werewolf's endearing wife. "Actually, I'm here because of Rafe. I had a message to deliver to him, but instead of taking it and letting me go, he decided to kidnap me and ask me ridiculous questions that I already told him I can't answer."

Missy grinned. "Now, that sounds like something either one of them would probably think was a really good idea. That's why we women have to function as the voices of reason in the world. So, have you already delivered your message?"

Tess nodded, her smile broadening.

"And he's received it, read it, and comprehended it as well as the male mind will allow?"

Tess nodded again.

"Well, then, I'd say your work here is done." Missy shot the men a pointed glance. "Would you like me to call you a cab? Or you're welcome to spend the night. We've got loads of room, and I'd love to get to know you better tomorrow when we're both more awake."

Tess grinned. "A cab would be great. I've got to go to the other end of the city, so I'd really appreciate the lift."

Rafe growled and crossed the room in four long strides until he stood directly in front of the couch and glared down at her. "I am not done with you yet. You will leave when I say you can leave."

Missy rolled her eyes and stood. "Oh, enough with the King of the Jungle routine, Rafael. It's late and there's no reason to keep the poor girl awake all night while you try to decipher the mysterious code of plain English I'm assuming her message was written in. Let her go. If you have more questions, you can always ask her tomorrow."

He shook his head. "No. This is not your business, Missy. This is a matter for the Council to discuss."

Missy shook her head right back. "The last time I checked, Mr. Lay-Down-the-Law, the Council had thirteen members, not two. So if it's a Council matter, you obviously can't make any decisions about it until you speak to the entire Council. And since that meeting supposedly ended at two, you're not going to be doing that tonight. I'm sure the rest of the Council is already home in bed by now."

Graham laughed, but quickly schooled his face

into more sober lines when his wife turned to glare at him. "Sorry, honey, but you're forgetting that almost half the Council is vampire. It's barely teatime for them. I'm sure the lot of them are still at the club drinking my brandy and telling lies about the length of their fangs."

Missy huffed out a breath. "You know what, sweetums? Next time, don't help."

Tess laughed, feeling much better than she had before Missy walked in, and stood. "No, I think Missy's right, Graham. It is late, and I do want to get home. I've done my job and delivered my message, and I have a real job I need to get to in the morning. So if you'll excuse me, I'll just thank you for the coffee and be on my way."

Rafe growled. "I don't think so. Tess, sit back down and be quiet until I tell you that you can leave."

She felt her eyebrow shoot up like a rocket. "What was that? I'm sorry, but I have this strange sort of deafness. I can never hear it when people are horribly rude to me. Would you mind repeating what you just said?"

"You heard me."

She stepped forward until her toes practically touched his and tilted her head back to glare up at him. "No. No, I really think I didn't."

She heard the snarl welling in his chest, but it was too late to back off now. She braced herself for his explosion, but it never happened. Instead, Graham stepped forward quickly and placed his hand on Rafe's chest to hold him back.

"Come on," the Lupine said as he nodded to his wife, who gently urged Tess back into her seat. "This isn't going to get anything done. Tess, please stay here for five more minutes while Rafe and I go see if we can round up the members of the Council. If we can, we'll talk this over real fast and give you an answer to bring back to the Witches' Council; if not, you'll get to go home, and we'll contact you tomorrow with our answer."

Tess pursed her lips. "I liked Missy's idea better."

"So did I," Missy said with a shrug, "but as compromises go, this one could be worse. Besides, now that I'm awake, I want a midnight snack. You can keep me company while I bug the staff at the club and wait for them to send something over for me. I really would like to get to know you better."

Tess looked at Missy's kind and friendly face, then at Rafe's harsh, set one. She sighed. "Fine. But if you aren't back in fifteen minutes, I'm out of here, like it or not."

"Deal." Graham was already dragging Rafe toward the door. "In the meantime, make sure my wife doesn't eat anything with chocolate in it. She's breast-feeding, and it gives the baby hives."

Four

"So," Missy said as she settled onto a bar stool at the island in the massive kitchen. A huge roast beef sandwich and an enormous glass of milk sat in front of her, recently delivered by a frighteningly efficient waiter from the club next door. "You said you have to be at work in the morning. What do you do?"

"I own a shop on West Ninth Street." Tess eyed the sandwich in amazement as Missy raised it to her mouth for the first bite. She couldn't believe this petite little woman actually intended to eat something larger than her own head. Although Missy Winters wasn't model-thin, she was by no means a heavy woman. By rights, any woman who called this gargantuan meal a midnight snack ought to weigh approximately seven billion pounds. "It's an herb-and-tea shop. The East Village Apothecary."

Missy chewed, swallowed, and blotted her lips daintily with a napkin. "How fabulous." She drained a third of the milk in one thirsty gulp. "How long have you been in business?"

Tess watched her bite off another slab of cow.

"About seven years. But the shop's been around since the 1970s. I bought out the previous owners."

"How old were you when you did that? Nine?"

Tess laughed and made a face. "Twenty-two. Don't let the Shirley Temple hair fool you. I'm older than I look."

"You must be, since you look about sixteen."

"Gee, thanks."

"Don't mention it." Missy finished the first half of her sandwich and grinned. "Sure you don't want some? Speak now or forever hold your peace."

"No, thanks." Tess shook her head and watched with wide eyes as Missy shrugged and bit into the second side of beef. "I mean, I really don't mean to be rude, but . . . how the heck do you eat like that and not outweigh your husband?"

Missy choked down a swallow of milk and laughed. "Don't do that while I'm drinking. You almost made me snort milk." She quickly cleared her throat. "And believe me, if I'd tried to do this six months ago, I probably would weigh more than Graham. But this is one of the best fringe benefits of having baby werewolves. I burn calories like a raging metabolic inferno."

Tess felt her eyebrows arch. "When did you have the baby? Last year?"

"Last month. Two weeks ago, to be precise. Well, two weeks and five days." Missy beamed with a proud-new-mama smile and downed another third of the milk. "A boy. Roark. I'd force you to come upstairs and meet him, but he was fussy tonight and now that he's finally asleep I don't want to risk waking him."

"Two weeks ago? You've got to be kidding." Tess gestured to the tightly belted robe at Missy's waist. "What did you do, adopt? Because two weeks is not enough time to lose a baby belly."

"That's the other fringe benefit." Missy pushed her empty plate away and sat back with a satisfied grin. "I told you, I burn calories like it's going out of style. Have since I first got pregnant. Werewolves have really fast metabolisms. They probably burn seven or eight thousand calories a day on average. They eat like horses. When they're breast-feeding, human women burn about five thousand. And I've just discovered, much to my joy, that when breast-feeding a baby werewolf, a human woman can burn somewhere around twelve thousand calories a day without breaking a sweat." Her grin widened. "Ain't life grand?"

Tess laughed. "That's a diet plan I don't think I've seen on the infomercials."

"Not in this lifetime. The Lupines—well, all the Others, actually—are trying to remain secret from the human world, but it's getting harder all the time. They're not about to go telling people anything about themselves until they've got absolutely no other choice."

"Is that likely to take much longer?" Tess asked, thinking of the conversation she'd overheard between her grandfather and the other members of the

Witches' Council. "I mean, I'm hardly an expert, but I think that might have been one of the things my gr—the council wanted to talk to Rafe about. I've heard some of the members rumbling about how some of the Others in the city haven't been keeping as tight a lid on things as usual. There were rumors about some Fae being spotted over the summer."

Missy sighed. "Yeah, that didn't exactly put the Council in a good mood. It was a huge mix-up, and we sorted it out as soon as we found out what was going on. But I suppose there will always be people who aren't happy with that. It makes me crazy, but it also makes me happy that Dmitri's Council position went to Rafe and not to Graham. Call me kooky, but I'd prefer it if my husband spent his time worrying about keeping me and the baby happy, not the entire Other population of Manhattan."

"I'm sorry. I didn't mean to offend you—"

Missy's scowl smoothed out into a warm smile so rapidly that Tess wondered if she'd ever really seen the angelic face wearing such a hostile expression. She must have imagined it.

"Oh, you didn't. I get carried away sometimes. I'm the one who should apologize," Missy assured her. "But that subject is no fun, anyway. I want to hear more about you. What sorts of things do you sell at your herb-and-tea shop? Besides herbs and tea, of course."

Tess shook her head and laughed. "That's the bulk of it. The herbs range from fragrant to flavorful, though most of what I have is medicinal in one way or another. I'm a licensed herbalist, so I make blends for specific problems people might have, and I tailor remedies to specific people."

Missy's eyes widened. "Wow, that's really cool. I've always found herbal medicine to be a fascinating subject. How did you get into that?"

"It's sort of a family business. My grandmother was an herbalist, too, though she just practiced for her family and her neighbors. She never made a career out of it."

As if Tess's grandfather would have tolerated his wife having a career beyond pleasing him.

"Cool. And you said you sell teas, too?"

Tess nodded. "Good-quality loose-leaf from all over the world. And I make up my own blends to sell as well."

"I'll have to come see you and try some. And maybe see if you've got something to put fussy, cranky baby werewolves to sleep a little faster." She rolled her eyes and laughed. "So that's it? Herbs and medicines and teas?"

Tess started to nod, then shrugged. "Well, I do readings, too, when things slow down. It's a nice extra income."

Missy looked curious. "What kind of readings? Tea leaves?"

"I don't have the patience for that," Tess laughed. "No, I read tarot cards. And the occasional palm. My grandmother taught me that, too."

"No way! Really?" Missy's eyes lit up like a teenager's, and she almost bounced on her stool with excitement. "Oh, now I definitely have to come visit. I've always wanted to have a reading done, but I never knew if I could trust any of those people who put signs out in their windows and call themselves Madam Juniper, or whatever."

"Some of them aren't bad. You just have to be careful, and take things with a grain of salt. Like, some people think tarot tells the future. It really doesn't, and anyone who says it does is lying. All it does is point out what sort of circumstances are happening around you and how those circumstances could turn out given your current way of thinking. It's totally changeable."

Tess shifted in her seat and felt one of her inner jacket pockets bump gently against her side, as if reminding her what she always carried with her. Some people kept emergency flashlights. She kept emergency divining tools. Probably because she was a witch, not a Boy Scout.

She looked at Missy and reached into the pocket. "Actually," she said slowly, "I have a deck with me now. If you want to see a really quick idea of what it's like."

Missy's expression took on a glow of excitement, and she clapped her hands together. "Oh, you wouldn't mind? I'd hate to put you out, but I would adore that. If you're sure you're not too tired?"

Tess shook her head and pulled out the velvet

pouch that held her favorite deck. "Not at all. I knew I'd be up late, so I took a long nap this afternoon. But since we don't know how long the guys will be, I won't do an entire spread. I'll just let you ask some specific questions and throw down a few cards to try to answer each one. If that's okay with you?"

The other woman nodded. "That's fabulous. Whatever works for you."

"Great." Tess handed the cards to Missy. "Then go ahead and shuffle these. Just play around with them and give them back to me whenever you feel like you're ready."

Missy nodded and began shuffling the oversize cards, a frown of concentration creasing her forehead. Tess waited patiently, letting her mind wander into the right space for a reading. After all the years she'd been doing them, it only took a minute. Contrary to what most people believed, tarot had a lot less to do with the supernatural than it did with psychotherapy. Reading cards didn't require magic powers, just a creative mind and an understanding of the ways in which people's brains worked. Tess had always found it to be a funny coincidence that she was both a witch and a tarot reader, rather than a given.

She accepted the cards when Missy passed them back to her, then twisted them in her hands so that the side that had been on the top when Missy held them was on the top when she held them as well.

"Great," Tess said. "Now go ahead and ask one question at a time, and I'll lay down three or four cards to try to get an answer. You don't have to ask out loud if you don't want to, okay?"

"Okay."

"All right. Tell me when you're ready."

Missy paused for a second, closed her eyes in concentration, then opened them again. "Okay. Ready."

Tess laid down the first card. The Queen of Swords. She felt her eyebrow twitch, and wondered what question Missy had asked. She had assumed the new mother would want to know something about her son or her own future, but Tess didn't really see Missy as the Queen of Swords type. She seemed too earthy and nurturing for swords. If she'd had to guess, Tess would have said Missy was a pentacles type. The Queen of Pentacles, perhaps, or maybe even the Empress card. If anyone was the swords type, it was Tess herself.

"The Queen of Swords usually represents a woman," she explained, "though it could be representing an idea or a situation. Assuming it's a woman, though, she's someone who is mature. Not necessarily old, but grown up. Not a kid. She tends to be intelligent and focused, maybe even a little cerebral. She approaches things with logic, and prefers to talk out a situation as opposed to attacking it. You might say she uses her wits first. Actually, *witty* is a generally good word for her. She can be willful, too, but in the upright position like this, she's not manipulative, which is good."

She looked at Missy to gauge the other woman's reaction, but the blonde just smiled and kept her question to herself, nodding encouragement.

Shrugging, Tess reached for a second card. Who knew what Missy had asked? Maybe the card made sense to her.

"The King of Wands. That could be your husband." She tapped the card with one fingertip. "If it isn't, Graham is still a good example of what this guy is like. He's mature—again, not old, but grown up—and generally very charismatic. He's energetic and successful and really charming. Probably too charming for his own good. The kind of man who just blazes through life on sheer force of personality. Like I said, either Graham or someone a lot like him."

Missy's mouth curved. "Yes, it does sound a lot like someone I know pretty well."

Tess smiled. At least that seemed like an appropriate card for Missy's spread. Then she flipped a third card and stared at it for a minute. So much for the "appropriate" idea. What the heck was going on?

"The Wheel of Fortune," she said slowly. "That's . . . interesting. One meaning is just what the card sounds like. It's the turn of luck in your life. Upright like this, it means good things are happening, and you're benefiting from them, which is great. But some people also think that when it shows up in a reading it signifies the influence of Fate on your life. That whatever is happening or about to happen

to you is something you really can't control. You just
have to ride it out and see where it takes you, because
that's where you're destined to be."

She hesitated and looked back over the two other
cards she'd already laid down. An uneasy sort of
feeling had begun to twist inside of her stomach. She
wasn't quite sure why, but she thought it might have
something to do with this impromptu reading. Her
hand hovered over the deck until Missy looked at her
and smiled her warm, comforting smile.

"Go ahead," Missy urged. "You said you'd set out
four cards on the question and see what they said."

Tess obediently reached for a final card, slipped it
off the top of the deck, and carefully turned it over.
The Two of Cups.

"Shit."

Missy looked at the card, then back up at Tess with
an amused expression. "What's the matter? It's not
like it's the Death card," she pointed out. "It looks
like a very pretty card to me. Isn't it a good one?"

"The Death card isn't really bad." Tess's reply
came automatically. Her eyes were still glued to the
fourth card laid out on the smooth, pristine counter-
top. "It just means change."

"Then what does this card mean?"

"True love."

"Well then." Missy looked from the card to Tess
as a beatific smile spread across her pretty face. "Isn't
that just perfect?"

Five

"Perfect," Rafe growled as he stalked beside Graham through the semi-hidden hallway that connected Vircolac to the library in Graham's neighboring house. "Thirteen bloody members on that bloody Council, and I still get stuck with the job of making contact with the witches."

"You are the head of the Council," Graham pointed out, sounding amused.

"And you are not helping."

Rafe's temper had not improved during the brief, informal meeting with the rest of the Council members. He had his suspicions about why the witches would want to contact the Others for the first time in nearly four hundred years, and none of the possibilities he had in mind made him very happy. The only good thing he could see coming out of the situation was having met Tess. And since she seemed not to consider him to be her favorite person at the moment, even that couldn't soften the entire blow of being caught up in this political mess. He growled.

"Look," Graham said, his tone carefully reasonable, "if we're right and the witches are considering breaking out of the Accord, it's important for us to talk to them before they do anything rash."

"I know." Rafe wasn't pleased about it, but he did know.

The Accord of Silence had been reached centuries ago, long before the split between the witches and the Others, even before humans had begun writing down tales about men who changed into beasts or cast spells to wither flocks and tell the fortunes of kings. Since the first time when humans began to realize there was something different about some of the creatures walking among them, witches and Others alike had relied on the power of the Accord to keep their existence separate and hidden from humans. It was a formal agreement that none of the races or powerful sects on earth would reveal their existence to humankind. To do so would be folly, but in order to preserve their secrecy, the cooperation of all supernatural creatures and magic users had been vital.

The idea that all of it might end because the witches were tired of hiding made him grind his teeth in frustration. That issue had supposedly been settled in 1627. Why would the witches want to rehash it now? How could they be so irresponsible as to risk the lives of so many non-humans just because they wanted the right to wear pointy black hats in public?

"Don't sound so grumpy or you'll scare the human," Graham said, grinning.

"She is not human. She is a witch."

"Last I heard, witches *are* human. So unless

they've been doing some experimentation that we Others haven't heard of . . ."

"Bite me."

"You're too old and tough. I'd much rather kick you out and go nibble on my wife." He paused, lifted his head, sniffed. "Who I see has been nibbling on something herself while we were busy. Roast beef, I think. With extra-hot horseradish. They're in the kitchen."

Rafe already knew that. He could smell Tess's sweetly pungent fragrance drifting to him from down the hall. He tried to resist the urge to inhale deeply, but failed, and then he had to snarl at Graham when he caught the Lupine eyeing him with an amused expression.

"What?" he snapped.

"Oh, nothing." Graham's grin belied his nonchalant tone. "It's just nice to see the man who once said he'd never be happy with one woman at a time be so focused on one woman."

"What are you talking about? Don't confuse me with one of your bloody packmates, wolf boy. You Lupines are the idiots who think mating with one person for all eternity is a good idea. We Felines know better, at least most of us do. We know that variety is the spice of life."

"But you didn't always."

Rafe gave his friend a warning glare. "Don't bring up that idiotic old wives' tale. There's no evidence to prove a word of it. No one in the last dozen generations has been able to remember a time when the spotted Felines mated for life. Leos and Pumas can do what they like, but Felines like me? We're cats, not bloody wolves."

"I didn't say a thing about it. I just think it's an interesting legend, don't you?"

"No."

"I mean, think about it," Graham continued, ignoring the way Rafe was baring his teeth in annoyance. "It's the stuff romantic movies are born of. A beautiful witch; the arrogant jaguar shapeshifter who broke her heart by sleeping with another woman just days after she'd promised her heart to him. The curse she laid on him that his progeny would grow fewer and fewer in number with every passing generation until they died out of this world, unless one man of his blood could find true love and remain faithful to her for a year and a day. That's a hell of a story."

"And that's all it is. A story. With no basis in fact and no evidence supporting the idea that it ever happened. Remember that."

"Who are you reminding, Rafe? Me? Or yourself?"

He shot his friend another scowl and stalked toward the kitchen. He entered through the swinging door to see Missy and Tess seated at the island counter looking at what appeared to be tarot cards. His eyebrows shot up as surprise momentarily took precedence over his annoyance. "What are you two doing?"

Tess jumped at the sound of his voice, her hand jerking awkwardly, the deck of cards striking the edge of the counter. She cried out as the cards scattered, landing all over the sprung-wood floor.

"You're a little jumpy," Graham observed, stepping into the kitchen behind Rafe and quirking an eyebrow. "Something the matter?"

Tess blushed and quickly shook her head. "No, I'm fine. Everything's fine. I'm just tired. It's late. I'll just pick these up and go."

Rafe bent down to help her retrieve the cards, scooping up a handful where they lay facedown on the floorboards. "You read tarot cards?"

"I used to," she muttered, snatching the cards out of his hand and shoving them into a little velvet bag the color of burgundy wine.

He looked at her, trying to puzzle out what she meant by that. Obviously, if she'd just been reading for Missy when he and Graham had walked in, *used to* had to be a fairly new development. He picked up another handful of cards and handed them to her.

"Well, at least they all seem to have landed facedown," he pointed out, trying to think of something to say that would calm her. When he saw his innocent observation make her stiffen, he realized he hadn't found it. "I mean, so you don't have to spend all that time flipping them over. That would be a pain."

"Right," she muttered, her eyes scanning the floor with frantic, darting glances. "A pain."

Rafe gave her a puzzled glance, then shrugged,

handing her a third pile of cards. He looked around to see if they'd gotten them all and spied one stray card. It must have fallen straight down the side of the counter without getting caught in any of the air currents that had sent the other cards scattering. Instead of falling facedown on the floor, this card had slid down the side of the island and gotten lodged upright in the tiny crack between the top of the baseboard molding and the side of the island. It stood up straight and colorful against the white wooden background.

"Looks like I spoke too soon." Rafe looked down at the full-color illustration with interest.

Poised on the edge of a cliff, ready to tumble straight over the edge and into the unknown, the figure on the card seemed at once jaunty and pathetic, totally unaware that he was about to leap into a situation that could easily spell his doom.

"That's an interesting image." He leaned down for a closer look. "A little unnerving, perhaps, but intriguing all the same. The baseboard is covering the caption, though. What is it called?"

When he got no answer, he turned his head to look up at Tess. She was staring down at the card in front of him with an absolutely stricken look on her face. Her skin was pale, her blue eyes were wide and dilated, and her lips had parted on a strangled gasp.

"That," she said, after a long pause and a couple of silent false starts, "is the Fool."

* * *

Tess stared at the last card in the deck and thought she heard the faint echo of Fate laughing at her in the background. More than anything in the world, she wanted to deny her suspicions and tell herself that it couldn't be true, that the reading she'd tried to do for Missy couldn't possibly have ended up being about herself instead.

There was no way the cards had decided to inform her that she was destined to have an affair with a passionate, fiery, charismatic man with an arrogant streak and enough charm to seduce the pink off a flamingo. A man who sounded a lot like Graham Winters, but—unlike the smitten, thoroughly faithful werewolf—one who remained unmarried and unattached. One who maybe had sharp, Latin features and melting golden eyes. They certainly couldn't be telling her she was the fool, poised on the brink of a journey that would change her life and leave her a different person than she'd been at the beginning.

No, that couldn't possibly be happening to her.

Except that it was.

She swore, silently but creatively, and snatched up the last card in her deck before shoving the whole thing into its pouch and the pouch back into her jacket pocket, where it would be safe until she could take it home.

And burn it.

"Um, thanks . . . for . . . everything," she fumbled, easing toward the exit, "but I have to—uh . . . I have to go now. Nice meeting you."

She darted out of the kitchen and down the hall so fast she'd practically reached the front door before she heard them launch into protests behind her. She was just reaching for the knob when a large, dark hand closed over hers and stopped her.

A dark head bent toward hers, and Tess found herself suddenly feeling small and vulnerable, surrounded by this man for the second time in one night.

"What's the matter?" His voice rumbled in her ear, low and rough and dark, and she fought back a shiver. "You look like you've seen a ghost."

Tess laughed. "No, I've seen ghosts before. They're not this scary."

"Then what is? I know you're scared of something, sweet Tess. I can smell it on you."

She closed her eyes and shuddered. "Do you have any idea how disturbing that is?"

He chuckled and nuzzled her hair. "You'll get used to it."

Tess's eyes flew open, and she shook her head emphatically as she fought back the panic that vow engendered. "No, I won't. I'm not going to get used to anything about you, because I'm going to leave this house and go home to my apartment and pretend that I've never seen you. I'm never going to see you again. In fact, I think that's going to become my favorite new hobby. Pretending that you just don't exist."

"You can pretend all you want, sweet Tess." His tongue darted out to rasp at the sensitive skin behind her ear, making her shudder. "That won't make it true. I told you in the alley earlier that I wanted to eat you up just as soon as I found out what you wanted with me. Well, guess what, Tess? Now I know. And now I'm feeling very, very hungry."

"Tough." She jerked away from his hold and tugged the front door open, darting down the steps as fast as she could. The Felix followed at her heels as if he didn't even have to make an effort. She growled in frustration. "Would you go *away*? What do I have to do to convince you I am not interested?"

Rafe smiled and continued to walk beside her as if they were out for a casual stroll. "If you want me to think that you are not interested, *gatita,* you're going to have to find a way to stop yourself from becoming wet every time I talk to you. You will have to stop your scent from heating and ripening with your desire. Until you manage that, sweet Tess, I am going to know that while your lips tell me to leave, your body wants me to stay as much as I want it myself."

She turned on him and let out a strangled groan of frustration. "My body also wants to eat three pounds of chocolate on the fourth Tuesday of every month. I don't let it have that, so what makes you think I'm going to let it have you?"

"I think it," he said, hooking one arm around her waist and pulling her to him until her hips pressed close against his, "because this is also what I want, and I do not believe in denying my body what it wants. I think it because this is more than desire, sweet Tess; this is a need, and I am going to give you what you need, *gatita,* whether you ask for it or not."

Then his mouth cut off her protests, and she forgot what she'd been about to say anyway.

Six

He touched her, and she felt every single one of her protests melting. Just like her knees, her spine, and a percentage of her brain cells she didn't even want to contemplate.

But none of that mattered, because the taste of him was the most perfect thing Tess had ever experienced, and the rest of reality ceased to exist when his hands settled on her hips and tugged her closer against him.

Tess wrapped her arms around his neck on a groan, her fingers burrowing into the thick silk of his hair and twining themselves in the strands. She heard him purring with pleasure and felt the rumble of it like distant thunder rolling through her. When he angled his head and deepened the kiss on a growl, she shuddered and forgot all the reasons why she'd intended to avoid this. All the reasons she'd thought of to tell Fate to take a hike and stop messing with her plans. Right now the only plans she had were to never, ever stop touching him.

Rafe didn't seem likely to object to those plans.

Not judging by the way his hands had settled on her ass again, like they had in the alley earlier.

The man seemed to have a thing for her ass, and used his grip to tug and angle her hips until she felt his erection settle into the groove between her legs. Tess moaned and, feeling benevolent, made it easier for him by pushing her feet off the ground, spreading her legs, and wrapping them around his hips.

She felt him shift to compensate for her weight, spreading his own legs and getting a firmer grip on her bottom. He shifted her higher and rolled his hips in a slow, lazy thrust, and Tess moaned against his mouth. He was driving her crazy. And this kind of crazy, she didn't even mind.

She did mind when he tore his mouth from hers and avoided her whimpering attempts to recapture his lips in a deeper, hotter kiss.

"Damn it, come back here!" she hissed.

"No." He turned his head and arched his neck to stay out of her reach, and the frantic tugs she gave to his hair, his cheeks, his ears, anything she could reach, seemed not to even register with him. She bit back a curse against all shapeshifters and their damned superhuman strength.

He reached up to peel her arms from around his neck, pressing them to her sides and trying to lift her away from his body. She clung like a barnacle, locking her ankles together behind his back and tightening her thighs to clamp herself in place.

"Yes!" She gave her own credible growl and glared

at him. "Now get back here and finish kissing me before I get cranky."

She hadn't expected him to move, and sure as hell hadn't expected him to move so fast. She didn't even have time to gasp before she found herself spun around and backed up against a wall for the second time tonight. Only this time, she thought it was a safe bet that the man pinning her there had more on his mind than asking her some questions.

He grabbed her wrists and slammed them up beside her head. He leaned forward, using his weight to keep her still, and rolled his hips against hers. She cried out as her clit throbbed to life beneath her jeans. Jeans that would probably have a huge wet patch between the legs if he didn't hurry up and get her out of them. She opened her mouth to tell him that, but he cut her off with a snarl and a sharp nip to her lower lip.

"Quiet. Not another damned word."

Tess felt her eyes widen, and she went still. She could see a hot, savage glow in his cat's eyes and suddenly remembered that for all this man's sophisticated appearance and urbane polish, inside he harbored a beast that could make dinner out of her entrails. And if that thought wasn't enough to get her hormones under control, she was a sad, sad woman.

"I'm sorry," she managed, though her breath still came in ragged pants.

"Oh, it is much too late for that, *gatita*," he informed her, eyes glinting. "You should have apologized back when I cared. Now I am far, far beyond such things. The only thing I want to hear from you is you screaming my name when I am inside you."

Her mouth opened then closed, and she swallowed convulsively. His hips rolled in another lazy, taunting thrust, and she had nothing else to say. Not a damned word. All she could do was moan at the pleasure of it.

At some point her eyes drifted shut against her will, leaving her unprepared for the heightening of every feeling. Each sensation—the rasp of his stubble against her skin, the harsh sound of his breathing against her ear—was so intense, she had to fight the need to beg him to touch her.

"You know that I am going to get inside you, sweet Tess. Don't you?" His tongue swept the pale curve of her ear in a rasping caress, and one of the hands that had moved back to her ass moved lower, sliding between her legs to cup her from behind. "I am going to take you until you cannot remember your name, until you cannot lick your lips without tasting me, until you make yourself hoarse from screaming my name."

Her hands clenched, nails biting into his shoulders. The heat and tension inside her threatened to snap, and she thought she might break in half along with them.

"Your only choice is whether you want me to take you here, where half of Manhattan can see you writhing in pleasure, or whether I take you in privacy, where I can touch you all night long with no interruptions."

His teeth closed on the sensitive skin at the curve of her throat and bit down, sending her desire into overdrive and making her body overflow with cream. "Which is it going to be, Tess? Here and now? Or in my bedroom until you cannot stand any more?"

In the end, it wasn't the idea of being seen that decided her. It was the knowledge that one quick encounter against the side of a building, while it sounded great right now, was not going to satisfy the hunger he'd created inside of her. She needed more.

"Home," she said, and cried out when he answered with a low growl and a hard shove of his hips. If there hadn't been so much cloth in the way, she would have climaxed right then and there.

Instead, she had to get her feet under her and try not to collapse on rubbery legs when he withdrew the support of his body. He kept one hand on her elbow, and that alone was probably more responsible for keeping her upright than her own wobbly sense of balance. He never said anything to her, just tightened those fingers around her elbow and began dragging her through the dark streets toward Park Avenue.

The very first cab he flagged stopped for him. In any other circumstances, Tess would have snorted at that and said something about the perks of power, but as it was she didn't think she could say her own name. She damned sure couldn't remember her address, so she let Rafe tell the cabbie where to go while she climbed onto the big werecat's lap and proceeded to try to undress him in the back of the taxi.

It was a surreal experience for Tess, almost like being drunk. There was one part of her mind still thinking clearly, and that part sort of stood back with its arms crossed and shook its head, while all her other parts attacked Rafael De Santos's clothing as if he were a tightly wrapped present on Christmas morning. She fumbled with buttons, tugged at hems, and was reaching for his belt when the cab screeched to a halt.

The sudden stop sent her tumbling off Rafe's lap and onto the floorboards. She sat there for a moment, panting and dazed, while the object of her lust climbed out and paid the cabbie. She stayed right there, too, until he reached in and hauled her out, swinging her up into his arms and striding toward the attended doorway of a posh uptown building.

She wrapped her arms around his neck for balance and set her spinning head against his shoulder, hoping the dizziness would fade before they got to his bedroom. She didn't want anything at all to interfere with her ability to sense and savor every single thing he did to her.

"Good morning, Mr. De Santos." A uniformed doorman with a studiously bland expression nodded to Rafe and ignored the fact that he was carrying a disheveled blonde with wide, unfocused eyes into the sort of establishment where these things tended not to happen. "Nice to see you again, sir."

"I'm not at home, Carson."

"Of course you aren't, sir." The doorman followed

them into the building and strode ahead to a set of gleaming elevator doors. When he pressed the UP button, the doors slid open immediately, and Carson reached inside, selected the twentieth floor, and stepped back. "Enjoy the rest of your night, sir."

Rafe growled something unintelligible as the doors slid shut in front of them, and the elevator started with a smooth glide upward.

Tess looked at the digital floor display above the bank of buttons and saw the difference between their current location and their destination. Even if she wasn't capable of mathematical calculations in her current state, she was cognizant enough to realize there was a large gap between the two. She turned back to Rafe, blinked once as if in slow motion, then dove for his mouth.

She caught his lower lip between her teeth and tugged at it, as if trying to pull his mouth into hers. When she released it, she went immediately back for more, nudging his lips apart and plunging her tongue inside to forage for his own. His response consisted of backing her up against the wall of the car, flipping open the button on her jeans, and sliding his hand inside her panties. Tess screamed against his mouth and bucked her hips against his hand.

He tore his lips from hers and swore, something low and savage and foreign. He shifted to brace one arm under her bottom in order to raise her higher while his fingers sliced through her wet folds to find her opening and thrust deep.

Tess threw her head back and screamed again. Two long, wide fingers speared into her, stretching her and filling her. The unexpected penetration made her mind fog and her muscles clench, and she sobbed for the breath he had stolen from her. Her hips tilted and her legs climbed higher, until her knees were clamped about his rib cage and his fingers had slid as deeply as they could reach. His wrist twisted, fingers screwing inside her, and she moaned in pleasure and need.

"God, yes!" she panted, lips parted and eyes squeezed shut. "More . . . touch me . . ."

He leaned closer, clamping his teeth on the base of her throat, growling like an animal. Then his fingers moved and began thrusting, establishing a rapid, driving rhythm that caressed her internal walls and drove her closer to the edge. She could feel her muscles bunching and tensing in preparation for climax, and she whined at the unbearable pleasure.

Her fingers clutched at his shoulders, creasing the fabric of his suit jacket and biting into the flesh beneath. If he'd been shirtless, she might have drawn blood, but she didn't care. Her body bowed in his arms, hips thrusting mindlessly against his hand. He shifted her again, his touch withdrawing momentarily and tearing a frantic cry of protest from her.

"No! More! Please, more."

She could barely understand herself, but she needed him to understand. She needed him to understand that she would die if he stopped touching her.

She would die.

Then his fingers slid back, three this time, thrusting deep inside her, stretching her entrance and driving her higher. She thought she might have screamed again, wondered vaguely if the elevator was soundproofed, then squeezed her channel around him and forgot everything else. She could feel her moisture flooding his hand and shuddered. The awkward confines of her jeans meant his hand cupped her mound while his fingers drove her higher, keeping him from the deeper penetration she craved. She whimpered and squirmed and tried to draw the breath to beg. But he twisted his hand and pressed his thumb against her clit and nothing else mattered because she shattered, blind and breathless, sobbing in his arms.

Rafe felt her climax, felt the ripples of her contractions gripping his fingers, and fought for every shred of self-control he could muster. He wanted to tear off her jeans, throw her to the floor, fuck her right there in the elevator car, and to hell with the rest of the building. But he also knew that once he got inside her, he needed to stay for a good long time, and he could think of better venues for that. Simmering, he let her ride out her orgasm as the car drew to a halt and the doors slid open.

Her eyes had closed, and he doubted it had even registered that the elevator had stopped moving. Her arms still clung to his shoulders, her legs still gripped him like a vise, and her body still pulsed with aftershocks around his fingers. He didn't bother to withdraw them as he carried her down the hall to his front door. There were only two other apartments on his floor, and if one of the residents happened to see, they could damn well deal. Rafe had no intention of removing his fingers until he could replace them with something infinitely more satisfying to them both.

He strode to his door and pinned her to the wall beside it, listening to the tiny whimpers she made every time his movements shifted inside her. Her face had the soft, dazed sweetness of an angel who had savored her fall, and he couldn't resist kissing her, claiming her swollen lips and bruising them with the force of his desire.

When he pulled away, her eyes fluttered open, fogged and unfocused. She blinked up at him while he reached his free hand into his pocket and withdrew his key. He saw her teetering on the drowsy edge of sleep and growled, shoving the key into the lock and forcing the door open impatiently.

"Stay with me, damn it. I'm not done with you yet."

He got no answer, but he didn't think she was capable of one. Growling, he peeled her off the wall and carried her through the doorway into his entrance hall. He kicked the door closed behind them with no care for the resounding crash. He looked down at her, saw her eyes drifting shut again, and roared in frustration. Damn it, she could not fall asleep on him now. Fuck the bedroom. He needed to get inside her in the next fifteen seconds before she drove him over the edge. His head jerked up and he looked around him for one frantic moment before he saw his opportunity.

She gasped, her eyes flying open when she heard glass shattering on the gleaming parquet floor. He saw sleepiness evaporate and grunted in satisfaction, causing another crash of debris as he swept his arm across the surface of the inlaid art deco console table in the middle of his entry hall. He saw her look around, take in the gleam of the mirror behind the table, the smashed vase of tulips, the puddle of water, and the litter of broken pottery, and dented silver at their feet. Then her gaze flew back to his and her eyes widened.

"Rafe," she began, looking uneasy and hesitant, and he snarled again.

"Now, Tess. I'll have you now."

He set her down on the edge of the table and pushed her backward, stripping off her jacket and sweater as she went. He heard her gasp at the impact of cool wood against her suddenly bare back, but he didn't care. He wanted her bare to him, and he intended to have her that way.

He followed her down, leaning over her and setting his teeth to the narrow spot that joined the cups of her bra. He sliced through it and the lacy fabric fell away, exposing her nipples to his avid mouth. He latched onto one immediately, curling his tongue around the hard little point and tugging it into his mouth to suck hard. He heard her cry out, felt her hands bury themselves in his hair, and he grunted in satisfaction. She tasted like spice and warm cream, and he wanted to lap her up until he lacked the strength to lick his whiskers.

"Rafe! God, how do you do this to me?"

He didn't answer, just set his mouth to her other nipple and drew on it just as fiercely. She moaned his name and cradled him to her, already shifting restlessly against him. His hands insinuated themselves between their bodies and attacked her jeans, yanking the zipper the rest of the way down and then peeling the heavy, clinging fabric off her hips. She helped him, lifted her hips off the table, raised her knees to bring them into reach. He snarled at the way it put the cloth like a barrier between them, but as he took her panties down, too, her bare flesh distracted him. He tugged the whole lot past her knees until he realized he'd have to step farther away from her to pull them the rest of the way off. And that was not going to happen.

Leaving the fabric tangled around her ankles, he braced her feet against the edge of the table and grasped her knees, spreading them wide to make room for himself. Then he grabbed her hips and pulled them forward until her bottom bumped against her heels and she perched there, completely open to him. He shrugged out of his jacket as if it were on fire and reached down to open his pants. He grunted in satisfaction when he felt Tess's hands on his shirt, fumbling with the buttons for a second before she uttered a frustrated cry and tore the fabric open. Buttons flew in all directions, clattering against the walls and the wood of the floor, but Rafe could see Tess's gaze glued to his bare chest and felt a swell of pride.

If both of them hadn't been so frantic, he might have taken a moment to savor the feel of her hands on him or the appreciative look in her eyes, but he couldn't wait another minute to be inside her. He yanked down his zipper and freed his erection, guiding it to her dripping entrance. Poised there for a brief moment, he looked down into her eyes and felt an unfamiliar wave of possessiveness wash through him.

"Mine," he growled, though he'd never said the word before in connection to a woman.

He felt his lip curl and his fangs extend, and he watched her eyes widen as he gathered himself. Then he drove hard and deep to her core with one heavy thrust.

She screamed and parted like liquid velvet around him.

"Yes," he hissed, coming to rest deep inside her, buried to the hilt in her tight, hot core. She felt like heaven. She rippled around his penis the same way she'd rippled around his fingers, with slow, hot pulses and the slick flood of cream he knew he wanted to taste before too much longer.

But not now. Now he wanted to fuck her until she came apart around him and he spilled himself in her honeyed heat.

Bracing his hands on the table beside her head and his feet on the parquet floor, he let his muscles gather and began to pull back from her clinging heat.

"Wait! Wait." She gasped and moaned, shifting restlessly beneath him. "Not yet. Can't . . . I can't. Not yet."

He growled and continued to withdraw, sliding through her wet channel with slippery ease. Or it would have been easy, if she weren't so tight and snug around him. Her body felt like a fist gripping him, and it was driving him crazy.

"You can. You will. Now."

He heard her moan, whimper, heard a breathless sob as her body struggled to adjust to him. He knew he should go easy on her, give her time to get used to him, but he couldn't. He needed her too badly to be kind. All he could do was try not to hurt her and make sure she came as violently as he intended to.

His hips stopped when she held just his tip inside her. He wanted to withdraw all the way so he could savor that first, maddening stretch as he entered her again, but he couldn't bear to separate himself from her heat. This would be easier on her anyway. Now that he was already inside, he could ride her harder than if he withdrew completely and forced her to take him all over again.

He stood there, muscles trembling, bodies linked by a precarious inch, poised on the brink of his next thrust with her body soft and pliant beneath him, but he wanted more. He wanted her to look at him. To watch him while he fucked her, while he claimed her. Ignoring the unfamiliar feeling of possession, he leaned down to bite her lip, to get her attention. Her eyes flew open, once again dazed and dilated, and struggled to focus on him.

"Eyes open, Tess." He order was gruff and harsh and he didn't care. "Watch me. Watch me taking you." She whimpered and shook her head, but she didn't close her eyes. He grunted and leaned more heavily over her. "Good. Now take me."

He thrust home with heavy force, spearing her so deeply he thought he could feel the back of her womb. She screamed and he froze, afraid he had hurt her, but her body trembled around him and her hips lifted toward him, so he relaxed and began to claim her in earnest.

Over and over, he thrust inside her, riding her hard. She felt so amazing around him, milking him, squirming and writhing beneath him. Her fingernails bit into his bare shoulders, cutting deeply, but the pain only egged him on. She cried out with nearly every thrust now, her knees gripping his hips as he drove high and hard inside her. He felt himself approaching meltdown and grabbed her hips to hold her still as he threw his hips harder against her. He battered into her, unable to be gentle, unable to hold back. All he could do was ride out the madness by riding her hard toward climax.

He felt it hit her unexpectedly. One moment she twisted and struggled beneath him, trying to get closer and get away all at once, and the next she clamped around him like a vise, arms, thighs, and body all tightening and gripping him to her. She screamed, the sound issuing hoarsely from her raw throat, and her body arched like a bow beneath him, coming up off the surface of the table until only her head and her hips supported her.

Rafe wrapped his arms around her, holding her steady while he continued to drive inside her. Thrusting was more difficult now, as her body struggled to keep him inside, but he forced through her resistance with half a dozen savage thrusts until the pleasure took him, too, dragging him over the edge of climax. He poured himself into her on a rough shout, feeling his very being drain out of him and into her tight, encompassing warmth. Then he collapsed onto her, pinning her to the hard table, thinking with a sense of dread and wonder that he hadn't nearly finished with her yet.

Seven

Tess kept her eyes closed and tried to figure out what the hell had just happened.

Well, aside from the most amazing orgasm of her life, of course.

Somehow her evening, which had started with a bowl of pasta and a seven-hundredth viewing of her copy of *Best in Show* on DVD, had ended with mind-blowing sex on the entry table in the front hallway of the apartment of a man she'd never met before . . . oh, three hours earlier.

The man in question turned his head, stubble rasping against her throat, and swept his rough, agile tongue along the tendon connecting her neck to her shoulder. Then he purred, and Tess felt the sound rumbling through her, from where his mouth pressed to her shoulder to where his erection still pressed hot and hard inside her.

Her eyes flew open. Still hard?

He stirred on top of her, inside her, and his hands slid down from her hips, over her legs, stopping when they felt the bunched fabric around her ankles. Oh,

God. She was still wearing her jeans. She felt her cheeks flame.

He murmured something against her throat, shifting his weight to keep her pinned while he tugged away her short boots and stripped her jeans and panties the rest of the way off. Now she was left naked beneath him, with only the scraps of what used to be a bra hanging from her shoulders. Oh, yeah. She felt dignified.

She tried to squirm away, but froze when she felt his teeth sink delicately into her shoulder and heard a rumble of displeasure. Apparently he didn't want her going anywhere. She lay still while his hands shifted from her to his own clothes. She felt the glide of fabric against her skin while he shoved his pants to the floor. He shifted inside her when he stepped out of the fabric, and she bit back a moan. Her sensitized tissues took every shift as a caress, and she felt herself flooding around him. He gave a pleased rumble and licked her shoulder.

Tess cleared her throat. "Um, this table isn't really all that comfortable." She squirmed and pushed at his shoulders. "Do you think you could let me up now?"

There was a brief moment of silence. Then Rafe lifted his head and gazed down at her with lazy cat's eyes. "Sure."

She felt his body slip from hers and drew a shuddering breath. Okay, step one. Now for step two. But before she could even attempt to put her feet on the floor and lever herself out from beneath him, Tess found herself lifted, flipped, bent forward, and penetrated. He had barely let her get her feet on the floor before he kicked them wide, pressed her hips against the edge of the table, and slid into her from behind.

"This is not up," she gasped, struggling to remain coherent even as her body urged her to surrender to the power of their connection. The traitor. Never before had Tess found herself at odds with her own physical being. Her mind told her that any further shenanigans with the werecat in the room would lead to bad, bad things.

Her body told her mind to get lost.

She heard Rafe groan above her and her head automatically came up. Instead of meeting a blank expanse of entry wall, Tess found herself unexpectedly staring back into her own wide, blue eyes.

She had forgotten about the mirror, but judging by the hot, feral expression on Rafe's face, he had not.

When he'd first carried her into his apartment, Tess had been a little too preoccupied to pay much attention to the decor, so the huge, gilt-framed mirror above the console table had barely even registered. Instead, she'd been too busy registering the feel of his hands on her and then his body inside hers. But now, bent forward over the very same table with her hands braced on the inlaid surface and a gorgeous, feral shapeshifter draped across her back, she found the mirror hard to miss. It was about six inches from the end of her nose.

Startled, she tried to pull away, to stand up straight and put some distance between herself and her reflection, but Rafe would have none of it.

He leaned heavily over her, his chest against her back, pinning her in place with his bulk. He even buried one of his big hands in her hair and used it to tilt her head until she had no choice but to meet her own startled, aroused gaze.

"Watch." His mouth pressed against her ear as he gave the raspy order. "I want you to see what it looks like when I'm taking you."

She moaned helplessly and watched as his dark form began to move behind her.

The woman in the mirror looked nothing like Tess. Her eyes looked wide and wild, pupils dilated, expression dazed. Her hair was an undisciplined tumble of curls, all sense of style long gone. Soft tendrils had become glued to her skin with the sweat of their exertions, and the rest of the unruly mop curled and bounced with the impact of his thrusts. Her pale skin looked slick and flushed with sweat and arousal, and it contrasted a bright, milky white against his darker bronze complexion. It made her look even more vulnerable and him, even more powerful.

He looked, actually, like a conquering barbarian. His dark, angular features were drawn and tense as he thrust himself deeply, then recoiled to thrust again. His own dark hair was damp and mussed from her fingers, and his skin gleamed hot and slick in the dim, golden lights of the entryway. His body curled around hers, chest pressing against her back, thighs braced against hers, hands braced against the table beside hers, caging her. And all the while, he plunged in and out of her like a piston, hard and deep and relentless.

Tess cried out and felt her eyelids drift shut. Her head dropped back against his shoulder, and she moaned in heated arousal.

"No! Eyes open." He punctuated the order with a hard thrust that nearly toppled her onto the table. Tess screamed breathlessly, her eyes flying open and meeting his in the mirror. He looked savage and dangerous, and she cried out again, in fear and desire. "Watch. Watch me taking you."

She couldn't do anything else, fascinated by the contrast of his big body overwhelming hers. She saw his hands shift from the tabletop and slide upward to cup her breasts.

"Watch your pretty breasts swinging while I fuck you." He pinched the taut nipples and she moaned helplessly. "Watch the way your body shakes under mine."

One of his hands released its grip on her breast and glided over her belly and between her legs, fingers scissoring around her clit and sliding through her stretched folds until he brushed her entrance. His fingertip rubbed against the tight ring of muscle, felt how it stretched to accommodate his thick shaft, and the caress made Tess burn. She felt her internal muscles clench and sobbed his name.

"Rafe! Please!"

He leaned closer, teeth tugging at her ear as his finger simultaneously closed over her nipple and her clit. "Watch," he repeated. "Watch your face while I make you come."

Then his fingers tightened, pinching delicate flesh and Tess screamed.

This climax hit her like a Mack truck, and it didn't slow down after impact.

She watched her own face in the mirror. Saw her lips part on the scream, saw her eyes go wide and frantic, saw her skin flush red. Then she couldn't see anything as the pleasure blinded her.

All she could do was feel.

The pinching pleasure-pain of the fingers on her nipple and clit. The hot, slick press of his bare skin against hers. The violent contractions of her womb as her body struggled against the overwhelming sensations. The brutal impact of his thrusts as he raced toward his own climax. It lasted for the rest of her life, and then she melted onto the table like warm cream. Her mind struggled to remember how to breathe while Rafe gave one last, hard thrust and began emptying himself inside her.

Eventually, he pulled out of her body—which made her wince and whimper at the same time—and peeled her off the entry table. She felt him swing her up in his arms again, but she didn't even have the strength to open her eyes to see where he was taking her. She didn't think she could survive another taking, anyway.

Her head bobbled against his shoulder as he carried her through darkened rooms deeper into the apartment. She felt the rush of cool air against her sweaty skin when he shifted her away from his body and laid her down on a set of cool, smooth sheets of incredibly soft cotton. She murmured in pleasure at the feel of them against her bare skin and stretched out, flexing sore muscles and testing to assess the damage. Nothing permanent, she was happy to note, and curled back onto her side to snuggle into a fluffy pillow.

She felt the bed dip as Rafe crawled in beside her. She frowned as a wisp of thought drifted into her exhausted mind and teased at her. She struggled briefly to recall what it was, then felt his arms curve around her waist and gave up. She let him pull her limp body back against his and sighed sleepily. She was warm and comfortable and more tired than she could remember being in her life, and nothing in the world sounded better than sleep. Giving up the struggle, she let herself slip into unconsciousness, lulled by the deep rumbling rhythm of a big cat's contented purr.

When Tess woke, she remembered just enough to know she wasn't in her own bed or her own apartment, but it took a few minutes of lying absolutely still and taking very deep breaths before she remembered any of the rest of it. The thing that finally brought it all rushing back was the feel of long, masculine fingers gliding up her thigh and toward an ache in a place that didn't usually ache.

Her eyes flew open and she found herself looking into the amused face of Rafael De Santos.

Oh, shit.

"Good morning." His voice sounded even huskier than usual, and she could feel it rasping over her skin almost like his clever tongue. "I thought about letting you sleep some more, but I wasn't sure if you needed to be at work."

He bent down and pressed a warm kiss to her lips, seeming to savor her sleepy, helpless response.

"What time is it?" she asked when he finally pulled away.

"Ten after ten." He grinned. "And if you are already late for work, I apologize, but I only woke up a few minutes ago myself. Something wore me out last night."

Tess cleared her throat and reached out for a sheet to pull over herself. There wasn't one. She looked around but couldn't find a single cover, so she yanked her pillow out from under her head and clutched it to her chest. She also pinned her thighs together to discourage the fingers that were currently wandering higher and higher up the sensitive patch of skin.

"Sorry," she mumbled, watching him warily. "I didn't mean to sleep so late. Actually, I didn't mean to stay at all."

He shrugged and flexed his hand to squeeze her

thigh. "It's just as well. I had no real intention of letting you go." Reaching out with his free hand, he tugged the pillow out of her grasp and threw it across the room. "I'm still not sure I will."

Her eyes widened as his head bent toward her now exposed breasts. When his hot mouth closed around a nipple, she yelped.

"Hey! Stop that!" She pushed at his shoulders, which he apparently misinterpreted as a cue to suck harder. She bit back a moan and tried to pretend her body was neither stupid nor masochistic enough to actually be getting wet for him. Again. "Are you insane? Get off me!"

He raised his gaze to hers without releasing her nipple and quirked one dark, eyebrow. She saw his eyes glint, but barely had time to get properly worried before his teeth closed delicately around the base of the peak and began to nibble.

"Ayiiiee!"

The noise came from her, much to her astonishment, since she wasn't quite sure how she had made it. In any case, she had one brief, astonished moment of desperate arousal before her pussy throbbed sullenly, bringing her to her senses. Burying her fingers in his hair, she spent a few minutes gathering her strength—the fact that she was moaning and cupping her breast for him like an offering at the time meant nothing—before she tugged hard enough to get his attention.

Rafe lifted his head, her nipple slipping from his mouth with a pop, and she stifled the urge to whine a complaint.

"Thank you," she said instead, mustering up a halfhearted scowl. "Now I think it's time you let me up so I can go home."

"Home?" Rafe dragged his avid gaze away from her glistening nipple and raised an eyebrow. "What makes you think I'm letting you go home?"

Tess stiffened. "Um, because I want to and there are laws?"

"What does that have to do with it?"

"A whole hell of a lot, considering it's the difference between whether or not the police come swarming around your building like a plague of locusts."

Rafe ignored her furious scowl and sat up. "Since no one is going to be calling the police, I doubt they will have any reason to come to my building and eat all the crops."

"I damned well will call the police if you don't let me go."

"How?" His tone was idly curious as he stood and crossed to an enormous closet, emerging a moment later with an enormous bathrobe and a pair of casual linen trousers. The robe he tossed to Tess and the trousers he pulled on, covering up a tragic amount of bare, bronzed muscle. "If I decide not to let you call the police, Tess, it is not as if you will be able to defy me."

Tess blinked at him, eyes wide, mouth opening

and closing with shock. "You mean—you won't . . . you're going to . . . you can't just . . ."

Rafe grinned at her. "Hurry up and put your robe on, Tess, before I get so distracted that I forget about making you breakfast." He gave her an arrogant, indulgent look and swaggered out of the room.

Tess stared after him for a good long minute before her shock faded enough to let the anger bleed through. Shoving her arms into the sleeves of the massive terry-cloth robe, she didn't even bother rolling them up before she snatched the phone off the bedside table and held it to her ear.

She didn't get a dial tone, but she did get an annoying masculine chuckle and the infuriating sound of, "I'm not stupid, sweet Tess. Now come out to the kitchen—where I have the phone off the hook, by the way—and have some breakfast. After last night, you can use the protein."

Click.

Tess slammed the phone down on a strangled scream and headed for the kitchen, fully prepared to do battle with an arrogant, troublemaking werecat.

She wasn't prepared for French toast.

She couldn't have been more than five minutes behind him, yet when she stepped into the gleaming pine, black, and chrome kitchen, he was already laying the first thick slice of batter-drenched bread onto a sizzling griddle. It wasn't possible. And it damned sure wasn't playing fair.

"What do you think you're doing?"

He looked up from slicing another slab of bread off a thick loaf of challah and smiled at her. "Making breakfast. Do you want syrup or jam with your French toast?"

She braced her hands on her hips and glared at him. "What sort of dirty rotten trick is this? How dare you!"

"How dare I feed you?" He shrugged. "I suppose I thought you would be hungry. I myself am starved. And waffles would have taken much longer to prepare, but if that is what you would prefer . . ."

"That's not what I'd prefer. What I'd *prefer* is for you to act the way you're supposed to, damn it. Stop being so nice!"

"I am not supposed to be nice to you? How am I supposed to treat you?"

"You know. You're supposed to act like a man. Tell me how much you enjoyed spending time with me last night, and you hate to rush me out because it makes you feel so sleazy, but you really do have an appointment in a couple of hours. And can you get me a cab? You'll definitely call me if your schedule clears up so we can have dinner tonight, okay?" She paused for breath. "Aren't you supposed to be the Don Juan around here? Shouldn't you know how to do all this?"

She watched as he dipped a slice of bread into the bowl, then held it up to let the batter drain off. His movements were economical and expert and rather annoyed. "I am afraid not. Somehow I must have missed the training in how to behave as an inconsiderate ass when I was becoming such a 'Don Juan.' You will just have to forgive me if I am unable to behave as a total prick."

"That's not what I said." She shifted her weight and burrowed her hands into the opposite sleeves of the enveloping robe. How had she started to lose the upper hand here?

"Actually, that is exactly what you said. Or at least what you implied."

"But it's not what I meant."

"Then tell me what you did mean." He set a filled plate down in front of her and handed her a glass carafe of syrup. He pulled out a stool on the opposite side of the island from the cook top he was working on. "And eat your breakfast while you clarify for me."

She sat down reluctantly and picked up a fork, more to have something to do with her hands than because of an actual desire to eat. She didn't say anything while he finished cooking his own serving and sat down beside her with an impressively heaping plate.

"All right, I believe I asked that you to eat your breakfast and explain to me what you meant. Would you care to try for one out of two?"

Tess glared at him and speared a bite of toast, swirling it around in a puddle of maple syrup. "I just meant that you're . . . not acting quite like I expected."

He swallowed a mouthful of breakfast and sipped from a huge glass of milk. "What were you expecting? For me to boot you out of bed the second I rolled off you?"

She squirmed in her seat. "Well, a little."

"You really think I am that sort of man?"

"You do have a—a . . . reputation, you know."

"*Madre de Dios,* Tess, if you thought that I might be so large of an asshole, why in God's name did you go to bed with me to begin with?"

Tess rolled her eyes. "Right. Like I had a choice about that."

His brows drew down as a dark storm front passed across his face. "Are you implying that I somehow forced you to have sex with me?"

"Of course not." She blushed, feeling a surge of guilt. She hadn't meant it to sound like that. Or at least, she knew it wasn't true. "We both know it didn't happen that way. But Fate is Fate. And when it comes down to it, there's not much use in fighting what's meant to be."

Tess stared at her plate while Rafe pushed his empty one aside and cleared his throat. "So you are saying that we were somehow destined to sleep together last night?"

"I can't say for sure that it had to be last night in particular, but I'd be an idiot if I tried to pretend that all the signs didn't point to it happening at some point. I just didn't see any point in waiting. I think I figured that if we got it over with, it would be a lot easier for both of us to relax from now on."

"Of course. As you look so much more relaxed this morning."

She opened her mouth to retort, but closed it again when she saw a decidedly odd look cross Rafe's face.

"What's the matter?" she asked instead.

He looked at her, his face a carefully blank mask. "Your cell phone plays 'Turkey in the Straw'?"

She flew off her stool and out of the kitchen so fast she should have left skid marks on the parquet floors. "Granddad!"

Eight

She sprinted toward the entry hall like it was an Olympic event, then wasted valuable seconds picking her way through shards of broken pottery in order to get to her denim jacket and the cell phone she kept in the inside pocket. She flipped it open just before the last strains of the square-dance classic faded from hearing.

"H'lo?"

Pause. "Tessa?"

"Yes, Granddad, it's me," she said, stepping gingerly back into Rafe's living room and checking the bottoms of her feet for shrapnel. "How are you?"

He ignored her question. "Is something the matter? You sound out of breath."

"I'm fine." She looked up when Rafe appeared in the doorway, but she didn't tell him whom she was speaking with. "I left my cell phone in the other room, and I had to run to answer it. Is everything all right?"

"I had called to ask you the same question." His voice cooled and began to take on the tone of disapproval and censure that was a Lionel Menzies trademark. "I expected you to call me first thing this morning to tell me how everything went last night."

"Last night?" she repeated, her mind flashing to the events she decidedly did *not* want to share with her closest living relative.

Rafe clearly intended to give her no privacy. Instead of leaving her to finish her call in peace, he perched on the arm of the living room chair nearest the entry and watched her with interest while he sipped from a mug of steaming coffee.

"Yes. Of course, last night," Lionel snapped into her ear. "When you were asked to deliver a message to the head of the Council of Others. Did this task prove to be another that was too complex for you?"

"No. Not at all."

"Then I assume you delivered the message without incident."

Tess pursed her lips and looked away from Rafe's curious stare. "I delivered it safely to the head of the Council, just like you asked." She didn't intend to discuss any of the details of last night's incidents for her grandfather. Especially not the ones that had happened right next to where she stood.

"And was there a reply?"

"A reply?"

Lionel sighed over the phone, his voice ringing with impatience and condescension. "Yes, Tessa. A reply. You were instructed to wait to see if their leader would offer a reply to our message. Did he give you one?"

Tess looked back at Rafe and saw him nodding. He was no longer perched on the arm of the chair, but stood in front of her, watching her intently and nodding meaningfully.

"Um, yes," she said, eyes fixed on Rafe's face. "Yes, their leader did offer a reply."

"And what did they say?"

Crap.

Tess frowned and bit her lip. She couldn't ask her grandfather to wait while she covered the mouthpiece and asked for Rafe's reply, because then she'd be compelled to explain why she was still with the shifter so many hours after completing her mission. But in the excitement of last night's events, she had totally forgotten about waiting for a reply from the Council.

Automatically, she stalled for time.

"They said . . . um . . . that is, they told me to tell you . . ." Desperately, her gaze flew back to Rafe for guidance, and she saw him once again nodding with deliberate meaning. "They, uh . . . they said, um . . . yes?"

Rafe grinned at her and nodded one last time. Tess blew out a relieved breath and turned her attention back to her grandfather's voice.

". . . like to see you as well. Is seven convenient for you?"

Tess caught the tail end of what sounded like an invitation and frowned. "I'm sorry, Granddad. There must have been a little static. I'm afraid I missed what you just said. Would you repeat it, please?"

Lionel sighed again. It was his customary response whenever Tess spoke to him. "I do wish you would listen more carefully, Tessa. I said that the council chairs would like to speak with you before the meeting in order to get your impressions of this De Santos fellow. I've invited them to dinner tonight, and I asked if you would join us. At seven, please. And be sure to dress appropriately."

Before she could accept or decline, Lionel hung up and left Tess scowling at her silent cell phone. *Invite,* her ass.

"You didn't tell me your grandfather holds a position on this Witches' Council," Rafe said, standing to guide her back into the kitchen. He filled a new mug with coffee and set it down before her. "I gathered that was the meaning of your phone call. The Witches' Council wished to hear my response to the message you delivered last night."

Tess nodded, wrapping her hands around the warm mug, but not drinking. "He doesn't actually sit on the council. Not anymore. He stepped down last year. But he is still active in the politics of it. Some of his close friends are still chair holders."

"Then they want to question you about me."

"Yeah, probably."

There was a brief silence while Tess contemplated the coming evening. Dinner at her grandfather's house always made her nervous, and dinner there with the inner circle of the Witches' Council would likely leave her with an ulcer before she finished her soup course. None of the council members had the slightest bit of respect for her, though considering that her grandfather had even less, she supposed she should stop feeling hurt by it. She'd earned her reputation for magical incompetence long enough ago.

"So what are you going to tell them about me?"

Tess's gaze flew to Rafe's face, and her eyes went wide as saucers. "Well, I'm certainly not going to tell them that!"

The Felix laughed, a deep, throaty rumble that echoed through the kitchen. "I didn't expect that you would. That's between the two of us." He winked at her. "I meant, what do you plan to tell them about your first impressions of me?"

"I can't tell them those, either," she mumbled. He heard her, though, because his grin widened and he chuckled into his coffee. Tess straightened. "I honestly don't know what they're expecting to hear from me. It's not like I know you all that well—"

"Other than biblically."

Tess ignored the twinkle in his eyes.

"—so I can't think what they're going to ask about. All I can tell them is that you seem pretty human, you're fairly intelligent, and you're friends with a werewolf Alpha. Oh, and you make killer French toast."

"I am fairly certain that those are not precisely the pieces of information they will be looking for."

"Me, too. But like I said, I don't know what they'll be looking for. Except to know that I probably don't know, you know?"

"I know."

Tess sighed and looked at her watch, then compared her findings with the digital readouts on his space-age microwave and built-in double oven. All sources agreed. She was way late for work.

"Look, thanks for . . . er . . . breakfast," she said, setting down her cup and cinching the belt of her borrowed robe even tighter, "but I really have to run. It's my assistant's day to open the shop, but I still have a ton of work to do. I should get going."

Rafe set down his own coffee and nodded. Stepping forward, he placed his hand in the small of her back and ushered her toward the bedroom. The move was old-fashioned and possessive and suited him like a layer of skin.

"Of course. Why don't you take a quick shower while I gather your things together? You will feel much more ready to start the day after you have cleaned up and dressed in your own clothing. All right?"

He didn't wait for her answer, just pushed her through the bedroom and into the master bath, showing her where to find clean towels, instructing her on the details of his state-of-the-art steam shower, and offering her his toothbrush. Then he smiled at her and left, shutting the door firmly behind her and leaving her alone in the sea of richly earth-toned tile and gleaming porcelain.

She blinked and reached for the shower faucet. Maybe he was right. Maybe a shower would clear her head. At this rate, it damned sure couldn't hurt.

Rafe waited until he heard the water start to run before he picked up the phone and dialed from memory.

"Yeah."

"Graham. I need you to find some information for me."

"Thank you for choosing the Silverback Clan for all your investigative needs. We sniff out all the news you need to know."

"Clever. You should get business cards printed up."

"I'm way ahead of you. The press had this really cool generic logo of a wolf baying at the moon, too. They're gonna be great."

"You had better hope Callahan does not object to you cutting in on his business. But in the meantime, this is important, and it needs to happen quickly. And with discretion."

Graham's voice snapped into serious mode. "Name it. I'm listening."

"I need you to find me what the community knows about a certain witch."

"I'm sure you do, bud, but you should know well enough that our kind knows not a whole hell of a lot about that crowd. They keep to themselves. They think we furries are nothing more than animals with opposable thumbs. If you want to impress the girl, you're going to have to get creative."

"Do not be ridiculous. This is not about Tess. I have a phone number for the witch in question, but I know little else." Impatient with the wolf's ribbing, Rafe flipped open Tess's cell phone and pressed a button to bring up her address book. Sure enough, memory slot number two read, GRANDDAD. He read the number back to Graham. "The name should be Menzies."

"Hm. No relation to your adorable little stalker, eh?"

"Just dig up the information for me. I will fill you in on the rest later."

Graham must have heard the impatience in his tone, because the Lupine grew serious. "You got it. When does this rush job of yours need to be done?"

"Before seven tonight."

Graham sighed. "Done. But you owe me, buddy."

"You know I will come through. Call me when you know something worth sharing."

He hung up just as the shower turned off. Standing, he tucked the cell phone back into Tess's jacket pocket and added the garment to the neatly folded pile of clothes in his hands. Then he schooled his expression into blandly pleasant lines and headed toward the bedroom. Maybe if he were fast and lucky, he'd get one last look at Tess's luscious little body before she left for work.

A man could dream.

Nine

Tess made it into the shop just after twelve thirty, partly because she didn't have to bother stopping home to shower, and mostly because Rafe had called a car service to drive her back to the East Village so she wouldn't have to take the subway. For that courtesy alone, Tess was prepared to forgive a multitude of sins, especially since the October weather had turned rainy and chilly sometime after dawn.

She thanked the driver of the town car, took him at his word that his tip was included in the service, and tried to ignore the way he stared very surreptitiously at her braless chest. She debated spending her day with her arms crossed over them, but wasn't sure that wouldn't defeat the purpose of circumspection. Instead she tugged her jacket more firmly shut and turned away.

Cheeks flaming, she headed down the five steps to her basement shop on West 9th Street. The sleigh bells over the door jingled as she entered, and the familiar, soothing smell of the shop greeted her as soon as she closed the door behind her. She inhaled the crisp, herbal fragrance and looked around for Bette.

"Well, well. Looks like I can call the National Guard and tell them it was a false alarm."

Tess turned to the back of the shop at the sound of the familiar voice, and she smiled. Elbows-deep in a huge paper sack of loose peppermint stood a young woman in her early twenties. Bette Beedle (her real name, Tess had learned, somewhat to her shock) had more facial piercings than she had fingers and wore her hair in a short, blunt bob dyed a vibrant electric blue. She had a talent for herbalism, a mind for numbers, and didn't mind working lousy hours. Plus, she possessed a warm heart and a great sense of humor, which was what qualified her to be Tess's one and only employee. "Sorry I'm late. It was a long night."

Bette grinned. "Ooh, that sounds promising. Was the cause of the long night long as well?"

Tess blushed. "What makes you think I'm late because of a man? Maybe I got caught up in a good mystery novel or something."

Bette sniffed the air, raised an eyebrow, and shook her head. "Nice try, but unless you've decided to switch from your usual lemon balm soap to—" She paused and sniffed again. "—mint, sandalwood, and myrrh, no dice. That's a hell of a nice masculine blend, though. Maybe we should try a new line of it."

"I don't think so." Tess started to shrug off her jacket and hang it on the coatrack behind the door, but thought better of it the second she felt herself shimmy. "I think it would be a better idea if we just finished up those custom tea blends for the Sanderson wedding reception, don't you?"

"No, but you're the boss." Bette finished emptying the last of the peppermint into a huge amber glass jar and screwed on the lid before replacing it on the shelf behind the counter. "So I guess that means you get to keep your naughty little secrets. Want me to go get the Sanderson trays now so we can get started?"

Tess appreciated that Bette took her refusal to talk gracefully, as she took most things, but it still made Tess feel a little guilty for being snappish. She shook her head. "No, that's okay. There's not all that much left to do for them. Why don't you take a break and go and get lunch. I'll watch the shop till you're finished, and we can do the Sanderson order this afternoon, okay?"

Bette shrugged. "Sure. I think I'm going to run down to that new café on Seventh. Want me to bring you back anything? They have killer veggie wraps."

"No, thanks. I had a big breakfast."

"I see. So you're back to taunting me about the secrets of your debauchery last night. Well, no matter. I'm a big girl. I can take it." She wriggled her eyebrows at Tess as she grabbed her coat and opened the front door. "But if I die of curiosity over my avocado-and-tomato sandwich, I hope you know who's to blame."

Tess laughed and shooed her out the door. "Get lost, you little drama queen. I'll see you in forty-five minutes."

Bette called out a cheerful good-bye and disappeared into the world above, leaving Tess in peace and quiet. Which, she soon learned, was not all it's cracked up to be.

She found that if she had something engaging to do, like bookkeeping, which required all her concentration and considerable cursing, she could go almost forty-two seconds in between thoughts of Rafael De Santos. If she tried to get by with just placing orders, filling orders, or organizing the shelves, she topped out at around fifteen. Which meant she had all her bookkeeping done twenty-five minutes after Bette left and was going crazy after another five.

When the shop door jingled for the first time that afternoon, it caught her once again staring into space like an idiot, with a dust rag in one hand and the other itching to touch Rafael De Santos one more time. Swearing at herself, Tess turned toward the entrance, glad of the distraction and more than a little curious. The apothecary did a good, steady business, but it wasn't the sort of store that drew crowds, and the five customers who piled into the shop at the same time definitely constituted a crowd.

"Hi," she said to the room at large, offering them all a smile. "Can I help you with . . . *Missy?*"

One of the women, a petite, curvy thing with auburn hair and dark sunglasses, laughed as she furled a black umbrella. "You're very sweet to offer, but if you want to help us with anyone, let it be Ava. We've been trying to find a way to deal with her for years, but no luck. Personally, I think Ava is beyond help."

Tess looked from the redhead to the slim, elegant woman in the tailored pantsuit and back toward the only face she recognized. "Missy? What are you doing here?"

The petite blonde smiled and hurried over to give her a hug and a kiss on the cheek. "You got me so curious last night that I had to come out to see your shop. I hope you don't mind. Especially since I told a few friends about it this morning, and they insisted on coming to see you and your shop for themselves."

Tess's eyes widened, and she shifted uncomfortably. "Um, just so I understand, what exactly about last night did you tell your friends about?"

Missy grinned and winked at her. "Why, that you own an herb-and-tea shop and give a mean tarot reading, of course. What else would I tell them?"

Those big, innocent brown eyes gazed back at Tess, twinkling so brightly that she instantly stopped wondering how this woman went about managing a man like Graham Winters. She clearly had the power to wrap him around her little finger without breaking a sweat. He probably thought his wife was sweet and innocent and malleable, too.

She snorted.

"I hope you're not too busy for us?" Missy asked. Tess looked pointedly around the small shop, empty except for her and Missy's friends. "Well, I think I can squeeze out a few minutes for you in between pressing nothings."

"Good. Then let me introduce you to my friends."

Missy smiled and turned toward the four other women. "Ladies, I'd like you to meet Tess Menzies. Tess, this is Regina Vidâme, Ava Markham, Danice Carter-Callahan, and Corinne D'Alessandro."

Tess offered each woman a smile in turn and made mental notes to help her remember who was who. Regina was the redhead who had made the joke about Ava, and Ava seemed to be the elegant model type with the silky dark hair and exotically shaped eyes. She was the sort that usually intimidated Tess, but at the moment, her expression looked perfectly pleasant, if a little remote.

It was odd, actually, because while Tess would have to say Ava was more beautiful than Regina, something about Regina's pale skin, auburn hair, and Mona Lisa smile gave her a striking quality Tess couldn't quite define. It niggled at the back of her mind while she turned to the other two women, quickly filing away that Danice had the gorgeous café-au-lait complexion and Corinne had the exotic Mediterranean coloring and features.

"It's nice to meet you," Tess finally said, nodding to them. "Did you all come in looking for something in particular?"

Danice snorted. "You might say that."

Missy stepped in front of her friend and gestured to the shelves of huge amber jars that lined the walls of the shop. "I just wanted them to get an idea of the sort of things you have to offer. Maybe let them sample a few of your blends."

"Absolutely." Tess never let curiosity keep her from making a sale, though she did look back at Missy and hoped she hadn't misinterpreted the woman's reassurances. "Let me put a kettle on, and we'll have some fun."

She kept an electric kettle on a shelf behind the counter, next to the sink and watercooler. Being able to brew up her wares for customers to sample made sense to her and had earned her a reputation for being friendly and accommodating. In the retail business, those qualities counted for a lot.

Getting the kettle ready only took a second, and when she turned back to her customers, she found them watching her intently. She blinked and stifled the urge to touch her hair. If they were staring at her wild, golden blond curls and thinking she needed to spend more time with a comb in the mornings, they'd just have to deal. Her hair didn't do tame.

Especially not after a night like this last one.

"So what sorts of qualities were you looking for?" She began scanning her shelves and pulling down jars, placing them on the counter. "I need to know if I have the right stuff."

She thought she heard a choking sound coming

from one of Missy's friends, but when she looked up, they all wore suspiciously bland expressions.

"Oh, we're sure you do," Missy said. "It's just a matter of getting you to show us."

Now, that sounded significantly odd. Tess shook her head and pulled out a mesh tea basket. "Okay, let's try it this way. Who are we aiming to please here?"

This time she was watching closely enough that she saw Danice's shoulders jerk and her hand come up to cover her mouth.

"Sorry," the woman said, looking not at Tess but at Missy. "Allergies."

"Well, that's a good place to start." Tess forged right through the odd energy in the room and reached for a jar of mullein. "Do you have high blood pressure?"

Danice gave a puzzled laugh. "Only when my husband is giving me grief. Why?"

"If you did, I'd be blending up a different formula. No ma huang with high blood pressure." Tess dragged out her small electronic scale. She laid a creased square of parchment paper on it and zeroed it out. "Does that cough ever go anywhere? Ever bring anything up, or is it usually dry like that?"

"Uh, dry?"

"And it ends up irritating your throat after a while, doesn't it?"

Danice's eyes widened and she stepped up to the counter to watch Tess more closely as she dipped into several jars, weighing each addition to the parchment with precise care. "Yeah, especially at night. I used to just blame it on the cigars someone is always smoking on the steps of the courthouse, but they instituted the no-smoking-within-a-hundred-feet policy and it hasn't really gotten any better."

"It will, but smoke is a stubborn irritant. Plus you sound like you're super-sensitive. It'll take a bit for your lungs to recover from the exposure."

"And in the meantime?"

"Well, if you like this tea, I'll make up a batch for you to take home. But try these, too." Reaching under the counter, Tess withdrew an opaque waxed-paper bag that rattled slightly when she set it on the counter. She smiled at Danice's curious expression. "Horehound candies. They taste pretty darned good, and they'll make your throat feel better and soothe your bronchi. Give 'em a try."

Tess automatically poured her herbal mix into a small pan, added water, and set it on a portable burner, but her eyes were on Danice. The other woman broke the seal on the bag and shook out one of the small lozenges, examining the rather unappealing brown candy with its powdery coating.

Tess grinned. "They're better than they look, I promise. The dust is powdered sugar. It keeps them from sticking together in the bag."

Giving her a doubtful look, Danice took a deep breath and popped the small candy into her mouth.

She sucked for a moment before her eyes widened. "Hey! These are pretty good. They taste sort of . . . maple-y."

"I add extract to the syrup when I make them. The horehound itself doesn't taste all that bad, but it's not exactly exciting, either. Take the bag. They really will help your throat."

"How much?"

Tess shook her head as Danice reached for her purse. "On the house."

"That's no way to run a business."

"Don't worry about it. If you like them, you can buy the next batch." She grinned. "Besides, I can always overcharge you for the tea."

Regina laughed. "Now I know why Missy likes you so much. You've definitely got the goods to handle . . . whatever crosses your path." She cleared her throat. "You got anything behind that counter to help a woman deal with a ridiculously Alpha male husband?"

"Sorry, but I don't think so. Well, not unless you want to try some damiana."

Reggie leaned her forearms on the counter and watched as Tess filled the tea basket with loose, black leaves and set it in a ceramic pot. "What's damiana do?"

"He'll be so busy thinking about sex, he'll probably forget about being king of the mountain for a few hours."

Corinne laughed out loud. "Oh, yeah. That's all

Reggie needs. For Misha to have an even harder time keeping his hands off her."

"I can always add some valerian. He won't know whether he's coming or snoring."

Her offer met with a brief silence, then an explosion of laughter from every party in the room. Even Reggie appeared to be smiling just a bit. "Um, thanks, but I think I'll pass."

Tess thought about the potential results of feeding Rafe some damiana and shuddered. After last night, she'd have to be insane to try and up that man's libido. Not unless she wanted to make it impossible for herself to walk for a week. "Right, then. That's totally understandable."

She grabbed the boiling kettle, half filled the teapot, then made up the rest of the liquid volume with the boiled herb mixture from the saucepan. A second teapot got a basket filled with pure Darjeeling, a few bits of lemon peel, and the rest of the water from the kettle. Carrying both pots over to the table in the back corner of the shop normally reserved for tasting, she plunked them down and crossed her arms over her chest.

"So," she said, leveling a glance at Missy. "Why don't you tell me what you're really here for and how much of what happened last night you shared with your friends?"

She watched as the other woman weighed her options carefully and seemed to choose ignorance as a tactic. "What makes you think we're not here for tea?"

Tess sat down at the table and poured herself a cup of Darjeeling. "You mean aside from the fact that you all are giving off so much nervous energy it's like being trapped in a room with twenty thousand hamsters on meth? Call it a hunch."

Missy paused for a moment before pulling out a chair and joining Tess for tea. "That's a hell of a hunch. You get those often?"

"Not as often as you're apparently going to try to avoid answering any of my questions."

Corinne flipped an empty teacup over and nudged it toward Tess to be filled. "It's a matter not so much of ignoring your questions as of easing into the answers."

"Is that what you call it?" Tess poured for Corinne, then lifted the other pot and poured a cup of the herb-and-tea mixture. She handed it to Danice. "I was just going to call it annoying. I mean, my first reaction is naturally to tell you to mind your own business, but since I think that's probably kind of rude—and since I also think I might genuinely like you all with a slightly better acquaintance—I figure rude might not be my best strategy."

Missy sighed. "Don't be mad, Tess. I really didn't tell them all that much about last night. I just mentioned that you and Rafe seemed to have a . . . connection of sorts. That's all."

Tess raised her eyebrows. "And for that, you all came down to the East Village in the middle of a workday in the rain? What makes this thing you seem to think Rafe and I have that important?"

"It's Rafe," Corinne announced. "He's been driving us crazy, so we've been keeping an eye on him."

"Well, it's Rafe, *and* the fact that we really like you," Missy added.

"And the fact that Rafe seems to really like you." Danice grinned over her teacup. "Or so I hear."

Regina nodded. "And then there's the fact that whatever you had to talk to Rafe about affects the Council as a whole, which means it affects our husbands."

"But really, it all boils down to the curse." Ava dropped that bombshell with her usual aplomb, then sat back in her chair and crossed her long legs. She saw her friends glaring at her and raised one elegantly arched eyebrow. "Well, it does."

Tess shook her head and looked at each of the women. "Okay, in order. One, why is Rafe driving you crazy? Two, it's not really anyone's business how much he likes me. Three, I know nothing about what I had to talk to Rafe about. All I did was deliver the message telling him the Witches' Council wants to meet with him. And four, what the hell? What curse?"

Missy shifted in her seat and set aside her teacup. She folded her hands neatly in front of her and said, "Look, Tess. Let me be blunt. I like you. I liked you from the minute I set eyes on you yesterday. I also like Rafe. He's one of my husband's best friends, and he's a wonderful man to boot, but he is driving us all crazy."

"How?"

"He won't settle down. Well, he seems to think he can't. What man wouldn't resist the idea of finding the right woman when he has such a perfect excuse not to?" Corinne rolled her eyes. "It's the dream of every male non-Lupine on the face of the earth."

Tess groaned and got up to throw handfuls of two new herbs into her brewing pot. She set it on to boil. "Okay, not only have you lost me again, but now you're giving me a headache. So please, speak slowly and use small words. At least until my willow bark is finished brewing."

Ava hooked one arm over the back of her chair in what should have looked like a sloppy, masculine sprawl. Instead, it looked like a *Vogue* cover pose. "I think we need to backpedal a little. The first thing we need to find out is how much our little Tess knows about shapeshifters in general and the Felines in particular. Then maybe we can pick the proper small words to get our points across."

"I know about as much as I found out talking to Missy last night. Which had more to do with human–Lupine procreation than with social customs." Tess saw Missy blush and smiled at her. "No, it was really interesting. It just didn't exactly leave me in the know."

"Didn't you learn any of it in school, or something?" Danice asked. "I mean, you're a witch, right? So don't you all just grow up knowing about all this supernatural stuff?"

What? Did they think she'd gone to Hogwarts or something?

Sometimes Tess forgot how ignorant humans could be not just of the Others, but of magic users as well.

"Afraid not. Witches are a bit . . . xenophobic, as a group. They know that a lot of things exist, but they don't see any point in actually going and meeting them. I'd heard shapeshifters existed, but the only things I've ever learned about them are from books and movies. And somehow I'm not sure Rafe has all that much in common with Nastassja Kinski."

"He's got a better body," Ava countered. "But no. I think we can safely assume that Hollywood has yet to render an accurate portrayal of any shapeshifting breed."

"Well, then I'm in the dark. Who wants to enlighten me?"

Everyone looked at Missy. She sighed. "Right. That's my job." She paused for a bracing sip of tea. "Okay, first of all, I should say I'm not an expert in Feline society. I'm not even an expert in Lupine society, and I live in that one. Part of the problem, though, is that Felines don't really have a society to begin with. The lions live in their prides, of course, but the different Feline species don't do a lot of intermixing. I suppose it's like us and the coyotes or jackels. All canines, but not all the same."

Tess reached for the willow bark tea and used it to warm up her Darjeeling. She nodded at Missy to continue.

"Just like wolves stick with wolves, the Felines mostly stay away from one another and maintain their independence, even when their territories overlap. In modern times they've gone ahead and appointed leaders in all the major cities just to keep the peace. They call each one a Felix, and he acts sort of like a Lupine Alpha. But that's where the commonalities end. I mean, we're basically wolves, and like most canines, we tend to live in groups with similar pack structures and social systems.

"But the cats are totally different. From what I've been able to pull out of Rafe and Graham, there are as many different kinds of Feline as there are big cats. Lions, tigers, panthers, leopards. They're all distinct species, and their Feline equivalents are all distinct groups as well. And just like the cats, werelions are the only ones with any sort of group dynamic among them. The others, like I said, tend to be loners and live separately. Which is probably why Rafe is the only Feline I've ever met."

Tess supposed that made a sort of really disturbing sense to her. Then again, maybe she was going off the deep end. "What kind is he?"

She winced, thinking that question sounded awful, but Missy didn't seem to take offense.

"A jaguar," the blonde answered with a smile. "I've only seen his cat form once, but he was beautiful."

"Careful," Regina teased. "Remember, you're a dog person, Miss."

"Okay, so that's the basics of Feline society," Tess said. "But what does it have to do with Rafe, me, and curses?"

"It has to do with . . . context." Missy shifted in her seat and fiddled with her wedding band. "When I say most Felines other than the Leos are loners, I mean it. There's some degree of variation, of course, but it's unusual to see more than one at a time without a fight breaking out, especially between males. And it means that Feline mating habits are different, too."

Tess fought down a wave of heat at the memories of the Feline mating habits she'd encountered so far. Praying her cheeks weren't on fire, she tried for a casual tone. "What do you mean by that?"

"Well, wolves mate for life," Missy pointed out, "and Lupines do, too. In fact, Graham says that in a lot of the shifter clans, there's some sort of permanent bond established between mates, even if it's a little less intense. From what I hear, the bears mate for life, too, and even most of the cats do it at least most of the time, like Leos and even tigers. Though I've heard the Tiguri—that's what they're called— form more political alliances than real mate bonds. Still, they stay with the same mate for life, according to Graham. But there are a few Feline breeds—like the leopards and cheetahs and, well, the jaguars—where they don't take real mates. They stay alone their whole lives."

Tess paused, digested. "Then how do they have little baby Felineses?"

"Not very easily," Ava said. "Which is where the curse comes in."

That little interruption earned her a glare from Missy, but Ava just shrugged, leaving Missy to explain.

"The curse is . . . ancient," Missy finally said. "It's a legend, really. No one remembers if things were any different before it happened, so . . ."

"Just spit it out."

"The legend says that things did used to be different with the Felines. According to the stories, all Felines used to mate for life, just like Lupines do. At that time their human and animal natures combined in such a way that they loved with the ferocity of the beast and the devotion of the man. But that was before. At some point so long ago no one is sure if it's fact or fantasy, a Felix from one of the spotted clans—some people claim it was a jaguar—supposedly met and became infatuated with a non-Feline woman. They had an affair, and the woman fell deeply in love with him. But after the initial burst of passion faded from their relationship, the Felix realized that he wasn't really in love with this woman, and he began to worry that a non-Feline mate would be unable to bear him the healthy cubs he wanted. So he left her to find a mate among his own people."

Tess felt her stomach twist a little. "Let me guess. She got kinda pissy about that, right?"

"She cursed him. Not just him, but all the spotted Feline clans. She vowed that if one male could be so fickle, so would they all. And until one male Feline of the same clan could change his spots and find a non-Feline mate to whom he could remain faithful for a year and a day, they would bear fewer and fewer children until all the spotted clans withered away."

"Gah! Did she sow their fields with salt while she was at it?"

"She does sound like quite the bitch, doesn't she?" Ava drawled. "Even I was impressed."

Tess shuddered and lifted her herbs off the boil, straining the liquid into a mug and adding a dash of straight tea and a lump of brown sugar. She stirred thoughtfully. "Okay, so I get the gist of the curse. I'm just still not sure what any of it has to do with me."

The five women at the table looked at one another, seemed to reach some sort of unspoken agreement, and turned back to Tess. She felt a little bit like a science fair project, some sort of strange bug pinned to a corkboard. She sipped her tea while she waited for an answer.

It was Missy who finally spoke.

"Well, you see, Tess, the woman who cursed the

Felines . . . she didn't just make it a non-Feline who could break the curse. She wanted her justice more poetic than that. She wanted a Felix to have to mate with someone just like her."

Tess arched an eyebrow and took another sip of tea.

"Tess, she was a witch."

Ten

It took Tess all afternoon to clean up the tea she'd sprayed everywhere after hearing Missy's final bombshell. She spent the whole time with a bottle of Windex in one hand, a wad of paper towels in the other, and a dazed expression on her face. Bette had tried to get her to confess what had upset her, but Tess just shook her head and kept cleaning. She didn't even really understand it herself; there was no way she could explain it to anyone else.

She went through the rest of her day on autopilot, filling orders and serving customers. And when closing time rolled around, Bette had the doors locked, the register counted, and the kitchen area cleaned before Tess even knew it was five.

"That's it, then." Bette shrugged into her coat and pulled out her key chain. "Everything's put away. I locked the back door, too, but if you're staying late, I can go run and unlock it."

Tess's head snapped up, and she shook it to clear away her fog. She glanced at her watch, saw the time, and shook her head. "Um, no, that's okay. I'm having dinner with my grandfather tonight, so I've got to run home and get ready before I head over there. I'll leave with you now. Just let me get my stuff."

She hastily put away her cleaning supplies, grabbed her jacket, patted the pockets for her keys, and then followed Bette out the front door. She started up the stairs and stopped when her assistant called her name.

"Hey, Tess! Earth to Planet Menzies. Were you planning to lock the front door tonight, or did I miss the sign saying, BURGLARY SPECIAL! COME ROB US NOW AND SAVE?"

Tess swore and jogged back down the stairs, but Bette was already using her key to lock up. "I'm sorry, Bette. I don't know what's with me today."

"Me, either." Bette pocketed her keys and urged Tess back up to the sidewalk. "At first I thought it was the aftermath of great sex last night, but now I'm not so sure. You seemed even weirder when I got back from lunch than you'd been when I left."

"I know. I'm sorry. It's just been . . . a really strange couple of days." Tess skipped right over the mention of great sex and hoped Bette would, too.

"Hm, well, as much as I'm dying to question you about that, and about the potentially great sex you had last night, I can't. I'm meeting my roommate at Veniero's for dessert debauchery before the show tonight. Her boyfriend's in a band. Along with the other three-quarters of Lower Manhattan." She gave Tess an assessing glance and sighed. "But I'm on tomorrow closing, so I'll get it out of you then. Just see if I don't. Bye!"

She hurried off down the sidewalk in the opposite direction from Tess's walk home and disappeared into the crowd. Tess sighed in relief. Right now, she had more than enough worrying her as it was. She did not need the Bettish Inquisition adding to it. Not when she was still freaking over Missy's news and scared half to death about the idea of having dinner with her grandfather and the high chairs of the Witches' Council. That seemed like plenty of worry for one person at one time.

More than, if you asked her.

She really tried not to stew about it during the twenty-minute walk back to her apartment, but of course, she failed miserably. It seemed a bit much to ask for her not to indulge in a minor freak-out over the idea that she might be the only thing standing between a species and its extinction. Especially given that donating to the World Wildlife Fund was not going to cut it. She still hadn't completely dealt with the idea that she'd slept with Rafe to begin with, so the thought that Missy and the others expected her to become his mate for a year and a day had her head spinning.

"It wouldn't be permanent," Missy had said. "It's not like we're asking you to marry him. Just . . . be nice to him. For the next three hundred and sixty-six days."

Tess could almost feel her eyes rolling back into her head again.

"It's not as if we're going to force you into it," Ava added. "We're not barbarians. We understand if the idea of spending the next year schtupping one of the most gorgeous men in Manhattan would be such a trial to you that you can't even stomach the idea. Just let us know, and we'll go let the Feline world know it was too much to ask."

At least Regina had protested that. "Ava, come on. Give the girl a break. It's not your responsibility, Tess, so don't feel like it is. And it's not like Rafe even knows about us talking to you. It was our idea, not his."

"Right." Tess scoffed at the memory, mumbling under her breath. "'Cause that makes me feel so much better."

She let herself into her apartment a little before six and wanted nothing more than to change into flannel jammies and sit in front of her television with a big bowl of popcorn and a four-pack of Guinness. Unfortunately, she only had forty-five minutes before she had to be out the door and hailing a cab to take her to her grandfather's house for the requested audience. If she rushed, she might have just enough time to make herself presentable to the point of passing inspection.

Lionel Menzies had really missed his calling as King of the Universe, instead becoming a successful investment banker, the same as his father and grandfather before him. But he still liked to call people into his throne room from time to time, just to keep his instincts sharp.

Tess, for instance, had been called upon the carpet

of his intimidating library so often, she thought she might have worn through the pile. Since Lionel had raised her after her parents' deaths when she was just four, she'd had ample time to try his patience and disappoint him on all possible fronts. She'd been mediocre in school, dropped out of college, and forgone a career in banking to open "that hippie dive in the ghetto." Unless she declared herself a lesbian, converted to Buddhism, and went to live in a commune in California, she didn't think she could fail more miserably in her grandfather's eyes.

Which meant dinner promised to be as much fun as elective root canal without anesthesia.

With such a fine incentive, she hurried through her shower, rinsing away the scent of Rafe's soap that had been driving her crazy since Bette first mentioned it. As soon as she stepped out and wrapped herself in a towel, she ruthlessly blow-dried her hair and set it in hot rollers to try to tame it. It never worked completely, but she was hoping to instill enough discipline to keep her grandfather from commenting on it the way he usually did.

While the rollers cooled, she slathered herself in lotion and pulled on bra, panties, and stockings before rummaging through her closet to find the Dinner with Granddad section—the one that contained all her most suitable and therefore least favorite dresses. She pulled one out without really looking and laid it out on the bed. They all looked alike to her, all with conservative cuts in traditional fabrics and dull, understated colors. She hated them all, so she figured it didn't matter which one she wore.

She tugged the dress over her head and padded back into the bathroom to take care of her makeup and finish her hair. The makeup took less than five minutes, but the hair decided to fight with her and took nearly fifteen before it settled into semi-respectability on top of her head. She gave it a securing spritz of hair spray and prayed for the best as she dashed back into the bedroom to grab her purse and slip on her shoes. She made it out the door at six thirty on the nose and prayed traffic wouldn't be too bad. She did not want to have to make excuses about being late on top of everything else. She thought her head might explode.

She was fairly sure it would by the time the taxi let her out at her grandfather's doorstep. After paying the cabbie, she paused for a moment on the steps of the elegant, understated brownstone and took a few deep breaths. She wasn't sure what they were supposed to do, but figured as long as she didn't hyperventilate it probably couldn't hurt.

She ignored the feeling of being stared at by random passersby and climbed the last two steps to the heavy brass doorknocker. She gave it a precisely spaced two taps and dropped her hand to wait.

The door opened, as always, in front of a moderately tall, moderately thin, moderately gray, and moderately polite man who had looked precisely the same age since Tess had been four.

"Good evening, Howard. I believe my grandfather is expecting me this evening."

"Miss Menzies." The butler bowed and stepped aside to let her in. "Mr. Menzies and his guests are in the drawing room."

Tess resisted the urge to roll her eyes and stepped into the foyer. Only her grandfather had a drawing room in this day and age. Of course, only her grandfather had a butler who could have posed for a treatise on stereotypes. Personally, she preferred her modest little lifestyle on the other end of the island. She'd rather be poor than pompous.

"Thank you. I'll show myself there."

"Very good, miss."

This time Tess did roll her eyes, but only after she handed Howard her coat and stepped past him. Not that she would have been surprised if he could see the gesture anyway. The man had strange and unsettling butler powers, made even more unsettling by the fact that he wasn't even a witch.

Tess paused for a second on the threshold of the drawing room—or the living room, as normal people liked to call it—before she convinced herself to just go in and get it over with. She figured if she approached this evening in the same way as she approached ripping off a bandage—really fast so the pain would be over and done quickly—she might just survive.

Call me an optimist.

Three people looked up when Tess entered the room, none of them appearing very pleased to see her. Not that she'd expected anything different.

"Good evening, Granddad. How are you tonight?"

She crossed to where the old man stood in front of the fireplace and extended her hands to him even as she reached up to kiss his weathered cheek.

Lionel Menzies was a tall man, a hair over six feet, and still had the posture of a general. He didn't bend down to make it easier on Tess.

"I'm fine," he dismissed. "Gentlemen, I don't know if you remember my granddaughter, Tessa. Tessa, this is Jeremy Knowles and William Bambridge."

Tess nodded to the two men, both of whom had been at her grandfather's seventy-fifth birthday celebration just six months ago. The one she had planned, executed, and hostessed. "It's a pleasure to see you again."

The men nodded at her and turned back to the conversation she had clearly interrupted. Tess sighed. She had known it would be that kind of night.

Rafe memorized the information Graham got for him before he left his apartment that evening, but in the end, his nose led him to her.

He followed Graham's directions to a very nice neighborhood on the Upper West Side, setting out once dark had fallen and making good time sticking to shadows and traveling silently through mostly deserted alleyways.

He preferred to remain hidden while he tracked her, since he hadn't told her of his intentions to spy on her during her meeting with her grandfather. Somehow, he didn't think she'd appreciate the gesture. He did not intend, however, to let that stop him from following her. After the information Graham had dug up on Lionel Menzies, Rafe wasn't quite sure he wanted Tess getting all that close to the man, blood relation or no.

According to the Silverback Clan's huge network of informants and observers, Lionel Menzies wasn't just a former member of the Witches' Council. He was the former High Authority, although he'd stepped down some time ago, rumors claimed he had merely gone behind the scenes, where he continued to manipulate people and events to suit his own purposes. And right now, his purposes had something to do with the Others.

Last night's note had certainly come as a surprise, and Rafe still hadn't quite been able to pin down the motive behind it. Why, after nearly four hundred years of diplomatic silence, did Menzies want to reopen relations between the two governing bodies? Why now? And why contact Rafe the way he had? Why not approach the Council as a whole, or approach Rafe personally? It wasn't as if Rafe would have turned Menzies away if the man had appeared on his doorstep.

Rafe shook his head and crouched deeper into the shadows. There was something odd going on here, and he intended to find out what it was. He had already agreed through Tess to appear at the next Witches' Council meeting, but until then he wanted to gather as much information about them as he could. It never hurt to be prepared.

He just wished he'd been more prepared for Tess.

Helpless, Rafe sighed as his thoughts drifted back to the same place they'd been all day—on Tess. Though come to think of it, that was right where he wanted to be, and where he intended to be again before the night was over.

Her taste had lingered in his mouth all day, and as soon as he'd scented her again this evening, his body had begun aching to have her. He hadn't been prepared for the power of his reaction to her. How could he have been when he'd never felt this way about another woman in his life? Tess was unique, and so was his response to her.

Rafe wasn't a man to put much store in legends. He considered himself a modern fellow, and he lived his life according to modern principles. He paid little attention to stories told by old men over pipe smoke and chessboards, but he knew something about his reaction to Tess set her apart from other women. Maybe the part where he didn't get bored with her the minute he'd had her. That might be a clue that she was different, but it didn't have anything to do with the ridiculous legend Graham had seemed compelled to bring up. Of that, he was sure.

He shifted restlessly in his hiding spot and tried to gauge the time. He'd arrived around eight thirty when Tess's scent had already begun to fade from the air, and he estimated he'd been waiting for somewhere just past an hour. He pushed aside a wave of impatience and sat back to wait some more. He wasn't sure just how long the meeting would take, but he was prepared for another hour at least. Either way, he would be waiting when Tess came through that door.

Graham had warned him that information on the Witches' Council was scarce, but what the Lupines had discovered painted an interesting picture.

Insular, secretive, and bordering on paranoid, the Witches' Council had been operating in Manhattan since just after the time of the last diplomatic relations between witches and Others. They had formed from the most respected elders of the community at the time, and created a sort of governing body to police the affairs of their own kind. Viewing mundane humans and Others alike with deep suspicion, the thirteen-member council—a bit clichéd of them, Rafe thought—saw to it that the secrets of true magic remained hidden from the outside world and that any crimes perpetrated by witches were answered by witches. It became a xenophobic little culture, simultaneously progressing with society and shunning it.

"From what I hear, they aren't fans of ours, either," Graham had said. "When they're not pretending the Others don't exist, they're letting their kids get their education about us the same way the humans do. Which is to say, not at all. They have some limited contact with Faerie, though. To tell you the truth, most of the good info I got, I got from Luc. You ought to talk to him yourself, when you have the time. He says he's met this Menzies guy—Lionel, by the way—once or twice. Doesn't seem all that wild about him, either. He called him, and I quote, 'an arrogant, unbending old bastard with a stick up his ass and the sense of humor of a three-day-dead golem.'"

Rafe tried to reconcile the image of Lionel that Graham and Luc had painted with what he knew of the man's granddaughter and found himself baffled. How in the world could someone as quick and lively and vibrant as the Tess he'd known last night possibly be a blood relation to a man like Lionel Menzies? Not only that, but have been raised by the man, according to Graham.

"He's her only living relative," the Lupine had reported with a grin. "Which means that when you petition for her hand in marriage, he's the one you'll be petitioning to. Good luck. Hopefully he'll take the news better than Missy's dad did. She still claims I nearly gave him a heart attack. Humans."

Rafe waited for the instinctive denial he always felt when someone uttered the words *marriage* and *him* in the same sentence. It hadn't come when

Graham had first said it, and it didn't come now. What was wrong with him?

He'd check himself for fever if it wouldn't make him feel like an idiot.

No, scratch that. He knew very well he had a fever. He'd been burning for Tess since the moment he saw her. Even when he'd taken her, he'd burned.

Shit. Something weird was happening to him.

Eleven

By the time Tess let Howard help her into her coat to leave, her face ached from maintaining her polite smile, and her jaw ached from being clenched for the past three-odd hours. If she didn't get out of her grandfather's house in the next fifteen seconds, she thought she might scream. She felt like she'd been questioned by the CIA, and thought she might just have the bruises to prove it. The mental scarring went without saying.

"Thank you for dinner, Granddad." She gave him a polite peck on the cheek as they stood in the foyer. "You didn't have to see me to the door, but I appreciate it. I'll call you next week."

Lionel waved that aside. "Yes, yes. I wanted to have the opportunity to remind you of what we said, Tess. Establishing a relationship with the Others is very important to us just now. The seers are certain that the time when we will all be exposed to society is drawing nearer. Unless we all band together now, we risk a very unfavorable reaction to our existence."

Since her grandfather, Senator Knowles, and Judge Bambridge had spent nearly every minute of the past three and a half hours impressing that very point upon her, Tess didn't feel she was likely to forget.

"I know, Granddad, and like I said, I got the impression that Rafe was not averse to the idea of speaking with you. I'm sure when he comes before the council, you'll all get things sorted out."

Lionel's head turned and his gaze sharpened on Tess's face. "Rafe?"

Tess swore at herself, and fought the urge to blush. Like that would go over well. "Yes. Like I said, I spoke to him and to several of his acquaintances last night. Rafe seems to be what he prefers to be called."

Lionel raised an eyebrow. "It sounds very familiar."

Not as familiar as I'm sure it sounded when I was screaming it last night—

"Don't be silly, Granddad." She lifted her wrist to glance at her watch. Pointedly. "Now it's getting late, and I have to open the shop tomorrow morning. I'm sure you'll forgive me if I rush home."

The mention of the shop had the desired effect. Lionel's mouth twisted in distaste at the memory of Tess's chosen career path, and he nodded briskly. "Fine. Just remember what we've told you, Tessa. We expect to hear from you if you have any further contact with De Santos or the Other Council members. Is that clear?"

"Perfectly," Tess assured him, nodding to Howard who opened the door for her. "I'll call if I hear anything, or failing that, I'll call as usual next Sunday. Good night."

Her grandfather didn't respond, but Tess considered that a good thing. She hurried down the stairs, taking her first deep breath when she heard the front door close behind her.

"God, I'm glad that's over!"

Her statement was accompanied by a low growl, too loud to be her stomach and too quiet to be a passing motorcycle. Besides which, her grandfather's cook had prepared an excellent rack of lamb, and the only traffic she could see on the street consisted of an elderly woman and the Pomeranian she held on the end of a six-foot leash. That growl had definitely not come from the Pomeranian.

Tess pulled her coat more snugly around herself and looked up and down the street. Between the puddles of light cast by the streetlamps, the sidewalks looked ominously dark and deserted. Tess snorted at her own fanciful thoughts. This was not the sort of block that deserved a description like *ominous*. Besides the fact that it was solidly upper class and well patrolled by the police, it housed three high-ranking witches, including her grandfather. It had wards up the wazoo.

Shaking off her paranoia, Tess shoved her hands in her pockets and turned toward the corner to catch a cab. If she was lucky, and the taxi gods were looking out for her, she might just make it home in time to watch the episode of *Good Eats* she had recorded before she called it a night.

She listened to the rhythm of her heels clicking against the concrete as she strode up the block. Maybe she listened too hard, because she didn't hear any-thing else. She certainly didn't hear the sound of a three-hundred-fifty-pound jaguar leaping out of the cover of two parked cars and herding her sharply into the mouth of a service alley.

If she'd had the breath, she probably would have screamed, so maybe that was why the jaguar made sure she hit the wall squarely between the shoulder blades, driving the wind out of her and rendering her momentarily breathless. It backed off as soon as it had her where it wanted her, sitting back on its haunches in front of her and watching her with intent golden eyes.

Tess stared at it while she struggled for breath, and it was the eyes that clued her in. Well, the eyes and the statistical chances of any other jaguars roaming the streets of Upper Manhattan on any given evening.

"Rafe?"

The jaguar didn't say anything, of course, because that would have really freaked her out, but it licked its whiskers and got up, crossing the narrow space sepa-rating them to nudge her hand with its broad, furry muzzle. She laid her wondering fingers on his skull and felt the rumbling vibration of the mother of all purrs coursing through him.

Oh, my God. It's really Rafe.

He stared up at her, amusement somehow clear in his feline expression. He looked like he was laughing at her, and the purr suddenly made Tess very suspi-cious.

"Get your chuckles while you can, buddy," she warned, though she couldn't stop her hands from stroking his thick, velvety pelt. "I'm going to get you for scaring me like that. You *will* pay for it."

He purred louder, and a long, familiarly rough tongue swept out to lave the inside of her forearm while she learned the textures and planes of his new form. He sat patiently before her while she stroked his head and shoulders, running her hands down his muscular back and legs.

He felt like velvet-covered granite, muscles hard and solid under her fingers, even more powerful than they were in the man. She found out quickly that he purred louder when she rubbed the base of his ears or stroked his throat or the incredibly soft patch of fur on his chest and between his front legs. When she tried to pet his tail, though, he pulled it away and she found it quickly wrapped around her, flicking teasingly against her legs.

She let out a deep shaky breath and stepped backward, dropping her hands while she tried to register how huge he really was. The top of his head came up to her breasts, and if he were to stand on his hind legs, he would have towered over her. His paws were nearly the size of her head, and his forelegs were almost as thick around as her thighs. He was massive and very nearly terrifying. If she hadn't spent all last night with him, she figured she'd be running away screaming right now.

At least for just about as long as it took him to

chase her down and rip her throat out with those sharp, white teeth of his.

Tess took a deep breath. "Okay, I'm going to assume you're here for some reason, like wanting to talk to me or something, but that's a little difficult while you're, um, furry, so how about you change back to normal, and we can go somewhere for a nice cup of coffee? Or saucer of milk."

The jaguar Rafe butted his head against her breasts, which nearly sent her sprawling, and then took her coat sleeve delicately between his teeth. He tugged until she took a few steps forward, then turned and padded toward the back of the alley. He paused there to look back at her.

She rolled her eyes, gathered her courage, and began to follow him. "If this is about Timmy being stuck in the damned well again, I'm going to turn you into a throw rug," she muttered. "Just see if I don't."

She heard a rumble that might have been laughter, but decided to ignore it as she followed Rafe deeper into the service alley. It was a darned good thing he knew where he was going, because Tess certainly didn't, and by the time they reached the end of the alley, she was following blindly. Reaching down, she buried her hand in the thick fur at the back of his neck and let him guide her around a corner and into another light-deprived alley.

Occasionally they left the dark to dart across a street, but in general they walked through the backside of New York all the way from her grandfather's brownstone to Rafe's modern apartment building. She noticed that this time, they didn't use the front door.

Rafe stopped at an unmarked entrance at the rear of the building and jumped up on his hind legs to bat an enormous paw against the service bell. Several seconds later, the door opened and a scruffy-looking young man wearing three days' worth of stubble and a pair of dark blue coveralls opened the door and looked down at them. He didn't say a word at the sight of a jaguar and a woman in heels and pearls standing at the door; he just stepped back and let them inside, holding out a key on a leather strap, which Rafe politely took between his teeth.

The jaguar stalked forward, easily navigating a narrow corridor to a dented set of elevator doors. He pressed the call button with his paw, and stepped inside the service elevator as soon as the doors dinged open. Tess followed, shaking her head.

"I guess you do this all the time. I wonder if the building has a no-pet policy?"

Rafe just sat on his haunches and watched her while the car climbed up to the twentieth floor. Three minutes later, they entered his apartment with the help of the key from the janitor. Tess actually took charge of that, snatching it from his mouth and fitting in the lock herself while she kept a weather eye on the other end of the corridor. She had every ounce of faith that Rafe could have handled it himself, but just then she wanted the security of a private, secure space and she wanted it as quickly as possible. She shoved open the door as soon as the lock turned and darted inside, slamming it behind them.

"Okay, two feet, De Santos, right now. Because I want some answers, and an enigmatic King of the Jungle stare is not going to cut it."

She heard another rumble of that feline laughter; then the air seemed to shift and shimmer in front of her. One minute she was glaring down at a stubborn three-hundred-pound jaguar, and the next she found out that the line of sight that put her eye-to-eye with the enormous cat put her eye-to-something-else-entirely with the equally intimidating man.

A naked, intimidating man.

Tess blinked, tore her gaze from Rafe's impressive erection, and found herself looking into a wicked smile as it spread slowly across his face.

"Oh, you'll get answers," he purred, and his voice sounded somehow even deeper and harsher than usual. "Right after I get what I want."

Tess's eyes widened, and she stepped backward, right into the edge of a very familiar console table. Jumping as if she'd been burned, she skittered out of Rafe's path and began backing toward the living room. "Just what is it you want?"

Then she pictured herself kicking her own ass for asking such a stupid question. Given which part of the man's body was currently pointed straight at her, you'd think she might have known the answer to her own question.

Duh.

Rafe's grin turned hungry and feral and savage.

"Guess," he purred.

Then he pounced.

Twelve

She darted away so fast, she wasn't quite sure how it had happened. Apparently her instincts were quicker than the rest of her because she managed to slip just outside his reach and go tumbling over the back of the sofa and onto the plush, art-deco-inspired carpet. Thank God the man didn't have a coffee table.

She landed on the carpet with an *oof!*—and quickly rolled to her side.

Before she could even get her legs under herself he was on her, leaping over the sofa and landing lightly beside her before he climbed on top of her and busied himself with peeling her out of her coat.

"Layers," he growled half under his breath. "Why the hell do you always have to be wearing layers?"

Tess sputtered and let him drag her coat off her arms to toss it aside because it gave her better leverage when she swung a punch at him. "None of your business! Now get your bloody hands off me, you jerk! I said I wanted answers, not a private screening of *When Creatures of the Night Attack*!"

He caught the blow easily and grabbed both her wrists in one of his big hands, pinning them to the floor over her head. He ignored her struggles, slipping his free hand under the hem of her conservative knit dress to grab the waistband of her panties.

"It is all right," he said, his tone casually cheerful. "We are currently running a special. Free attack before every conversation. Just sit back, relax, and enjoy the show."

His hand tightened, and he ripped the panties off her, tossing them behind him. Then he began to push her skirt up toward her waist.

Tess gave a strangled scream of frustration and tried to kick him, but he had already settled between her legs, so she wasn't landing anything anywhere that would do her any good. He ignored the blows pelting the backs of his thighs and pushed her skirt the rest of the way up until it pooled at her waist and out of his way.

"If you lay a frickin' hand on me, you asshole, I swear to you, I will—"

"Scream?"

He released her dress, shifted his body, and plunged two fingers to the hilt inside of her.

Tess screamed.

Her head flew back, and she found herself staring blankly up at the white plaster ceiling while her body arched and bucked under his hands. Those two fingers filled her full, reaching tender places that ached to be touched and making her flood his palm with thick cream. It stole her breath, leaving her aching for more. His fingers flexed and shifted, beginning to plunge in and out in a fast, relentless rhythm that made her desperate.

His touch drove her crazy, but what she really wanted was him, to be joined to him, his big, thick erection stretching her to the limits of endurance, then driving her hard over the edge. She forgot all about her irritation, her questions, and her identity, other than as the body currently pressed to the floor beneath Rafael De Santos.

"That's it, baby," he murmured, thrusting deeper, flicking his thumb over her straining clit. "Christ, you feel good. Hot and tight and wet around my fingers. You drip with cream for me. I want a taste."

She cried out again, almost in protest, but she didn't fight when he released her hands and slid down her body until his shoulders pressed her knees wide apart and she could feel his breath on her damp, swollen folds.

"Rafe!"

He answered her with a long slow lap of his tongue, from one end of her slit to the other. She screamed and bucked under his steadying hands. The warm, rough texture of his tongue drove her crazy, driving her up the slope of arousal and leaving her panting for more. Her fingers flew to his head, burying themselves in his hair and holding him to her while his tongue dipped into her and began lapping up her cream.

"Good," he growled, voice sounding rougher and harsher with need. "Sweet."

Lick. "Rich."

Nibble. "Hot."

Thrust. "Want more."

Tess gave him more. She didn't have a choice. Her body had taken over, no longer operating for herself, but for Rafe. She breathed, moved, existed solely for the pleasure he provided and for the moment when he would ease himself into her body.

"Please." She tugged at his hair, trying to drag him out from between her legs and up over her aching body. "Please, Rafe. I need you so badly."

He growled in answer and drove his tongue deep inside her. She screamed in pleasure, but it just made her redouble her efforts to pull him away. She wanted him inside her. Now. Before she died.

Desperate, she braced her hands on the floor and heaved herself backward with all her strength, leaving an unsuspecting Rafe staring at her ankles and growling ferociously. His head snapped up, and he glared at her, his golden eyes bright and savage with lust.

"No more playtime," she panted, holding out a hand when he shifted to his knees and began to stalk toward her on all fours. She could see the echo of his jaguar self like a mirage shimmering behind him, and she shuddered but stood her ground. "If you want to lay a hand on me again, it better be after you're inside me. Understand?"

"Be careful what you wish for, *gatita*," Rafe growled, low and menacing. "Because you are about to get it."

He leapt for her again, but this time she wasn't backing away. She met him halfway, returning every desperate kiss, every frantic caress. She felt him tug at her dress, yanking the fabric from her waist to her shoulders so he could see her breasts. His eyes fixed on her nipples, and he gave a hungry growl, reaching for them.

She slapped his hands away. "No. Not until you give me what I want."

"Fine," he growled, seizing her hips and lifting them off the floor. He sat back on his heels and tugged her into place, maneuvering her like a doll until he had her where he wanted her—with her ass perched on his thighs and her knees settled against the small of his back, digging into the sensitive flesh. It hurt, but she couldn't have cared less.

She braced her hands on the floor while he swung her legs up high, hooking her ankles on his shoulders so that when he leaned forward, he forced her knees back against her chest, bending her almost in two. He set one hand on the floor beside her head and reached between them with the other to grasp his shaft. Looming over her like a great, dark shadow, he bared his fangs and growled.

"You want me, sweet Tess? Then take me."

He drove deep with one hard thrust and sent Tess over the edge before she even realized she was teetering.

He didn't slow down for her climax, just leaned against her folded legs and began thrusting wildly against her, riding her through her crisis. She thought she might have begged him to stop—not that she wouldn't have killed him if he'd tried—but he ignored her. His hips worked like a piston against her, slicing through her tight sheath to reach the heart of her, then gliding back and plowing into her again.

When she slumped weakly to the floor, too wrung out and breathless to do more than lie there and accept his thrusts, he just growled and kept up the steady, possessive rhythm. Her legs slipped off his shoulders, and he caught them in the crooks of his elbows, keeping them spread high and wide for him. His eyes burned like yellow flames above her, and she felt the unbearable friction against her internal walls beginning to force her back up toward another peak.

She began to struggle, anxious to get away, not from him, but from the pleasure-pain of his possession. No one in her life had ever made her feel like this. She hadn't even known feeling like this was possible, and it terrified her. She could see, behind her tightly closed eyelids, the absolute perfection of their togetherness.

In that moment, she knew, with a certainty that went beyond tarot cards, beyond magic, to the fabric of destiny itself, that this man would be the air in her lungs until the day she died. He went beyond being her lover or her mate to being the one person in all the world who could make her whole for the rest of her life. The beauty and terror of the knowledge filled her, and she cried out, shaking her head in denial.

Rafe roared, shoulders hunching, arms shifting to force her legs even wider for him, as he thrust even more fiercely into her welcoming pussy. "Eyes open, Tess. Look at me. Look at me, damn you!"

Her eyes flew open and locked with his just as he gave one last, mighty thrust and began to pour his seed inside of her. She stared into those pools of molten gold while her body came apart in his arms, and she knew she would never be the same again. From now on, she would be his.

Whether either of them liked it or not.

Rafe came back to himself feeling simultaneously like he'd been beaten within an inch of his life, and like he'd just told a roomful of five-year-olds that there was no such thing as Santa Claus. How one man could feel so beat down and so bloody evil at the same time was beyond him, but that's how he felt.

He shifted gingerly and found Tess still lying beneath him, and judging by the feel of the pile beneath his hands, they still lay on the living room carpet like victims of an 8.0 earthquake. He shifted again and heard her groan softly. Shame flooded through him, and he began to ease his weight off her.

She looked pale as cream and still as death as she lay there, eyes closed, beneath him. The only sign of life he could see was the rise and fall of her chest as she drew in shuddering gulps of air and the glistening tracks of moisture that slid down her cheeks and into her bright golden curls.

He felt his stomach clench.

"Oh, *gatita,* I'm so sorry," he whispered, reaching for her but snatching his hands back before they touched her soft skin, afraid of hurting her even more. "Sweet Tess, I swear I never meant to hurt you. Come on, *querida.* Open your eyes and look at me. Let me know you will be all right. Tess?"

She shuddered and laid a hand over her eyes, shoulders shaking as she struggled to catch her breath.

Rafe swore. "Shit. All right, stay right there, *mi corazon.* I will get a blanket to wrap you up in, then I am taking you right to the hospital. *Christos, gatita,* I am so sorry."

"Sheesh, will you calm down, you big baby? I'm fine." She lifted her hand from her face and smirked at him, looking more amused than traumatized. "You didn't hurt me—well, not really—and it's not like I didn't ask for it. Hell, I think you made me beg for it before it was over. So chill, okay?"

"Chill? You are not hurt?" Rafe felt his tension deflate like a popped balloon. He thought his sigh might sound like one, too. "You are not hurt. All right. All right, I am sorry."

This time he did reach out and touch her, tucking a stray curl back behind her ear and stroking his thumb over the curve of her cheekbone.

"You are not angry with me?"

She shook her head. "Not about the sex. But we have more than sex we need to talk about."

"Right. You need to tell me about your meeting with the Witches' Council members."

"No. You need to tell me what the hell is going on, and why you were lying in wait for me when I left Granddad's house." She crossed her arms over her chest and glared at him. "I don't spill till you do, buddy."

Rafe grinned. He couldn't help it. Her expression appeared so fierce, but with her dress bunched up under her arms like that, she looked too ridiculous to take seriously and too cute for words. When her eyes narrowed, he schooled his expression into more sober lines and reminded himself she probably didn't want to know he was struggling to take her seriously. That was the kind of thing his Tess would certainly take exception to.

"Right." He scooped her up in his arms and got to his feet, feeling a surge of pleasure at the way her arms automatically curled around his neck to hold him close. "And I will spill whatever you want. Just as soon as I get you into a nice, hot bath."

She rolled her eyes at him. "Would you stop treating me as if I were made out of glass? We had rough sex. So what? In case you hadn't noticed by now, I like it when we have rough sex. Now will you stop trying to coddle me—"

"It's a Jacuzzi tub."

"Oh. Okay, then. We'll talk about it in the bath."

Thirteen

She would never admit it to Rafe, but the bath did feel wonderful. She could practically hear her sore, aching muscles sighing in relief as he lowered her into the steaming water. And when he turned on the jets, she was too busy whimpering happily to mind that he climbed in behind her without so much as a word and pulled her back against his chest. The tub was more than big enough for two, after all. Whether it would be big enough for the two of them and the erection she could feel swelling against her back was another matter entirely, but she'd give it the benefit of the doubt for now.

Her head fell back to rest against his shoulder. The water swirled and bubbled around them, and the damp heat made their skin stick together. It felt like heaven. Tess murmured in pleasure as Rafe lathered a washcloth and began dragging the nubby fabric over her skin.

"Now why don't you tell me about dinner tonight, *gatita*."

Tess opened her eyes and sighed. "I'd really rather you tell me what the deal is between the Council of

Others and the Witches' Council first. That way I might have a clue about what parts of dinner tonight were important."

"But I am bigger." He nipped at her earlobe. "That means I get to decide who goes first. And I have decided that you should."

"You realize it's the mark of a barbaric mind to use your size to try to intimidate me."

"I do."

She sighed. "I really don't get it. Why don't you all just forget about using me to spy on each other and have your meeting already? Wouldn't that be a whole lot easier and more straightforward?"

Rafe rubbed the washcloth over her stomach and flicked her earlobe with his tongue. "Who else was there aside from you and your grandfather?"

She sighed, trying to sound as put-upon as possible. Which was very, considering how painful dinners with her grandfather usually were.

"Jeremy Knowles, Republican, New York, and William Horatio Bambridge the Fourth, New York State Supreme Court."

"Hm. These men are both council members?"

"Yeah." She arched her neck when he began to nibble down the side toward her shoulder. No sense in making things difficult. For either of them. "Knowles holds the current chair as High Authority, and Bambridge holds everybody's dirty secrets."

"There is always one of that type." He nibbled his way across her shoulder, laving the skin in his wake. "What sorts of things did they ask you to tell them?"

She steeled herself against an attack of shivers. "I don't remember. Once they broke out the rubber hoses, things get a little fuzzy."

He bit down and growled.

"Ouch! Sheesh, if you're that hungry go fix yourself a snack." She jerked away and turned halfway around to glare at him. "They asked me what I thought about you, where you took me, what Graham seemed like."

She paused and changed her voice to a mumble, her gaze shifting away. Suddenly not even the sudsing water could make her feel clean.

"If I used magic to read you."

The silence in the room sounded louder than the tub jets. No one moved for a long minute, then he took her chin in his hard and forced her eyes to meet his. His gaze searched hers.

"Did you?"

"No! Of course I didn't. I don't do that kind of thing. Magic isn't there to be used like a pair of psychic X-ray glasses."

She scowled at him, offended, and he smiled back at her. His gaze had softened.

"I am happy to hear you think that way. Not everyone is so ethical, I am sad to say. Think about it, Tess. How many people who have the power to do something they want to do also have the power to resist the temptation to do it?"

"What, you think all witches are unethical?"

He hesitated. "I never said that."

"You didn't have to!" Tess scrambled to her knees and crossed her arms over her dripping chest. "You're nearly as bad as they are, aren't you? You think that anyone who's different or separate from you must be somehow morally lacking. What is it with men?"

Rafe blinked and shook his head. "Ah, I think I missed a step in your trail of reasoning somewhere. How did we go from talking about what happened when you had dinner with your grandfather to accusing me of racism?"

"You're the one who accused me of being all amoral and sneaky and manipulative."

"No, I did not do that. As I recall, I simply asked you to qualify a statement you had already made." He raised an eyebrow. "I think I would remember if I called you amoral and sneaky and manipulative. Because those are not at all the first words that come to mind when I think of you, *gatita*."

She tried to maintain her scowl, but he stroked a hand down her water-slicked thigh, making her shiver.

"My mind strays more toward words like . . . *luscious*. And *tasty*. And . . . *lickable*."

He suited actions to words, leaning forward and tracing his tongue along the seam between her hip and thigh. When she felt his breath against her damp curls, she jerked away and nearly fell backward into the water. He caught her before she hurt herself, and

Tess found herself pinned between his hard body and the hard porcelain of the tub.

"Let me go."

"No." He shifted his weight to keep her in place. "We have not finished talking yet."

"Haven't we? Because I told you everything I know, and you seem determined not to tell me a damned thing. So what else do we have to talk about?"

"It's not that I don't want to tell you things," he began.

"Then try doing that. It'll be a refreshing change of pace, at least."

He sighed. "I would have preferred you not be in the middle of this."

"Oh. My. God. Don't try to pull that protective crap with me. You put me in the middle the minute you started asking me questions about my grandfather, the same way he did by asking me questions about you! Sweetheart, I can't get any more in the middle than I am right now."

"All right. But let's get you dry first." Rafe pushed himself out of the tub then reached in to scoop her out, wrapping her in a fluffy towel before knotting another around his hips.

Tess gave a wistful look back toward the tub and sighed when he turned off the jets.

"Minx," he laughed, pushing her out into the bedroom and out again toward the living room. "Do not worry yourself. I have plans for that tub, too. We will get to those later."

"Spoilsport."

"Perhaps, but right now I am a hungry kind of spoilsport." He deposited her on the couch and headed back into the kitchen. "Would you like anything to eat?"

"I just came back from dinner!"

"Does that mean a yes, or a no?"

Tess rolled her eyes. "No. Thank you."

"All right, then. I will return in a moment. Why don't you go ahead and light a match in the hearth? The fire is all laid out; it only needs to be lit."

She found the matches on the mantel where everyone should keep some, she thought, and struck flame to tinder, watching as little fatwood sticks began to burn. The small fire began to give off heat almost immediately, and she settled into the chair closest to the hearth to wait for the werecat with the munchies. When he returned, he carried a tray piled high with sandwiches, pretzels, what looked like oatmeal raisin cookies, and a ginormous glass of milk.

"I said I wasn't hungry."

Rafe looked up from setting the tray on the end table beside her chair. "That is why I brought nothing for you."

He missed the widening of her eyes as he settled himself down on the carpet near her feet and reached for a sandwich.

"Now," he said, lifting the food to his lips, "what exactly do you know about the Accord of Silence?"

"I know what it is. It's the agreement under which

all Others and magic users have agreed to keep their silence to avoid being recognized by human society at large."

Rafe nodded and popped a pretzel nugget into his mouth. "Correct. It has operated for nearly fifteen hundred years now, but there are rumors starting to float around that it might not survive another fifteen months. Some groups are even advocating that it be done away with entirely so that the witches and the Others can begin to take a . . . more prominent role in world affairs."

"You mean there are a few crazy Others out there who want to take over the world."

"In plain speaking, yes."

"Okay, I get that." She nabbed a pretzel and crunched into it. "I mean, I don't get it, but I get it. But what I mean is, why now? And why is the idea such a bad one?"

She cut him off when he started to answer.

"I can guess that the idea of werewolves being your kid's gym teacher and vampires and witches moving into the neighborhood might upset some humans, but aren't they going to have to find out eventually? Fifteen hundred years is a damned long time to keep a secret. By now shouldn't there be enough witches and Others in prominent positions in society to cushion the blow somewhat?"

Rafe nodded. "There nearly are. More than a few people, myself included, believe that the time when humans are going to have to learn about us is not very far off. Whether we like it or not, we cannot hide forever, but the preparations that have begun are simply not sufficiently complete. We need another year or two to hedge as many bets as we can. And that is why the Accord is so important right now. Without it, we will lose control of our own revelation. And that could backfire on us. Badly."

"I'm not sure the Witches' Council feels any differently." Tess tucked her feet up in the chair under her and frowned. "From what I gathered from Granddad, they've foreseen the same thing. He mentioned that some of the seers on the council believe that time is coming very soon. Maybe even sooner than you do."

Rafe drained the last of his milk and licked the stray drops from the corners of his mouth. "Then we should have a very smooth meeting when I appear before them."

She studied his expression. "But you don't think that's going to happen."

"I do not."

"Why not?"

"Because something strange is already happening. People are beginning to believe in things they would have dismissed as their imagination even five years ago. A Fae friend of mine said that his wife's newspaper received nine thousand calls in a ten-hour period this summer, all from people reporting having seen an elf or a leprechaun. The *Times* recently ran an article on Manhattan's best spots for 'vampire and wolfman sightings.' Those are all signs that humanity might be closer to the veil than we think, and that they may even be developing the ability to see through it."

"Even I can't see through it, and I'm a witch."

Rafe raised an eyebrow. "Do not take this the wrong way, *gatita,* but you are the least magic-using witch I've ever met."

She made a face at him. "How many witches have you met?"

"One," he admitted, "if I count you."

"So how would you know how much magic I should or shouldn't be using?"

He shrugged and grinned. "I suppose I would not, would I?"

"Right. Mr. Smartypants." She tossed a pretzel at his head and laughed when he caught it in his mouth. "That's the problem with cowans. They all think—"

"Cowans?"

"Non-witches," she clarified. "They all think we walk around waving our magic wands or wrinkling up our noses every time we want to fill the teakettle. But magic isn't like that. It's not about making life more convenient for yourself. It's about exploring the mysteries and serving the greater good. Or at least, it should be."

"Does that mean you will not clean my apartment by making the broom dance across the floor?"

"I'm not cleaning your apartment at all. Hire a service. Though I'm sure you already have one." She shook her head. "Yeah, I probably could pull a *Fantasia* if I wanted to, but I'd be abusing the magic, instead of using as it was intended to be used. Not that I'm not occasionally tempted to put a hex on someone, mind you."

"No boils," he insisted, shuddering. "You can turn me into a toad if you must, but no boils. Skin conditions are much too . . . yucky."

Yucky?

Tess snickered. "I'll try to remember that."

"If you do not use your magic to clean your dishes or to make all the traffic lights turn for you, what do you use it for?" he asked.

Tess shrugged. "I suppose it depends on what sort of magic you have. It's not all the same, you know. Some witches couldn't do a hex if their lives depended on it, and some could turn your private parts twelve shades of green without breaking a sweat. Granddad is a spell caster. If someone has written it down, he can cast it. He's amazing."

Rafe stood, scooping Tess up in his arms and taking her chair, then settling her down into his lap. "What sort of magic do you have, then, *gatita*?"

She grimaced. "Not much, if you ask most people."

"I did not. I asked you."

She never had been able to explain her magic worth a darn, not even to other witches. Maybe that was one of the reasons why her grandfather had never understood, let alone appreciated, her talents. She had no idea how to make Rafe understand the energy that lurked inside her, but she took a stab at it because he had bothered to ask.

"I see things, usually stuff that's about to happen," she said. "Not like a real seer does. I don't have visions, or anything. Sometimes I just know the way things are going to work, almost like it's been blocked out for a play or something, and I've already rehearsed it. And I don't see it ahead of time like a real seer, either. It's usually just a few seconds, like fast-forward déjà vu." She made a face. "It's not really all that impressive."

His gaze on her was intent and inscrutable. "I do not agree with that. I find the idea fascinating." Then he grinned, and she braced herself against the charm of that look. "But let us try a little experiment."

"It almost never works on command." She tried to push aside the twinge of disappointment she felt that he'd dismissed her so easily. Not that she could blame him, really. Most witches found her meager talents just as uninteresting.

"Humor me."

He rose abruptly to his feet, carrying her with him, lifting her high against his chest. She gasped in surprise. "Where are we going?"

His grin curved like a pirate's, and a chuckle purred out of his chest.

"You tell me," he said, darting forward to nibble her earlobe. "Then tell me what is going to happen once we get there, because I believe it will only be a few seconds before it does."

Tess laughed and shook her head, her disappointment not standing a chance against the feeling of arousal that the look in his eyes ignited inside her. "Please. You could at least make it challenging."

He carried her through the bedroom door with a low growl. "It would be my pleasure."

Fourteen

"Hey, you've got something. Right here." Graham set down his burger and pointed to the corner of his mouth, nodding meaningfully at Rafe. "Looks kind of like a canary feather."

Rafe froze with his hand halfway to his face and glared at his luncheon companion. "Very funny."

The wolf grinned. "I thought so."

"With a new cub to care for, I advise you not to quit your day job for a place on the stand-up circuit."

"Come on, lighten up," Graham urged, munching on a french fry that drooped under its burden of ketchup. "You'd think a week of witchy sex would put you in a better mood."

"My mood is fine."

Actually, if he ignored the irritant of his friend's teasing, Rafe had to admit his mood was more than fine; frankly, he hadn't felt so contented and relaxed in years. If ever. He might not have swallowed any canaries in fact, but the smile he perpetually wore these days did conjure up the image of a cat who had. When he had met Graham at Vircolac before lunch,

Missy had even called his expression a smirk, but Rafe couldn't seem to rein in the smug curve.

It was all Tess's fault.

The little witch bore complete responsibility for his recent state of bliss. Her and her sassy tongue and her tempting little body. They haunted him, distracting him from his work, from his play, from his duties to the Council. Everywhere he went, he pictured her big blue eyes laughing up at him, or her sweet, pink lips pursed in irritation. Every time he thought of her, his palms itched to touch smooth, satin skin; and every time he caught a whiff of her creamy, lemon-herb fragrance, his mouth began to water.

Quite frankly, it was getting embarrassing.

"Your mood is distracted all to hell," Graham said, cutting into his thoughts. "I mean, don't get me wrong; I'm happy to see you enjoying a little of the good life, but I've asked you the same question three times now, and you still haven't given me an answer. I'd offer to let you go visit your little witch to work it out of your system, but if it hasn't happened by now, I don't have much hope for that strategy."

Rafe scowled. "What do you mean by that?"

Graham rolled his eyes. "Come on. We all know you're just the latest victim of the scourge known as woman. Misha even won the pool that guessed you'd go in an entirely non-Other *and* non-human direction. Me, I had you pegged for a sweet little lynx. Someone a little hard to get, but still in the cat family. Now I'm out fifty bucks. Which means you're totally buying lunch."

"Was I supposed to understand any of what you just said?"

"Don't pull that aristocratic blizzard tone on me. I've known you too long." Graham crunched up a napkin and tossed it onto his bare plate. "Look, none of us was looking for a mate when the right woman came along. Sometimes this shit just happens. There's nothing wrong with admitting you're ready to settle down. It happens to the best of us. And quite frankly, there are certain consolations, if you know what I mean."

Rafe tried to ignore the contented purr of his inner cat at the idea of settling down with Tess. Or better yet, on top of Tess. Pinning her down offered the distinct advantage of preventing her from trying to leave him.

And that was the craziest thought he'd ever had. Where had an idea like that even come from, for God's sake? He was a cat, not a canine. His sort didn't do the "settling down" thing.

He sent his friend a glare and drained the last of his beer. "I still have no idea what you might be talking about. I cannot even be sure that you know. Perhaps all those years of being led around by your nose have finally rotted your brain. I am a jaguar, not a puppy dog. I am not looking for a warm bed and a snug-fitting leash. I leave that to your sort."

"Yeah, that would be a lot more convincing if my nose wasn't telling me that you crawled out of a very specific warm bed this morning. Again. The same one that you've been crawling out of for more than a couple of days now."

Rafe felt his brows draw together. Yes, he had managed to convince Tess to allow him to stay at her apartment last night, but he had returned to his own home to shower and change hours before he had met Graham for lunch. He should have smelled of little more than his own brand of soap.

"Once again, I do not know what you are talking about."

Graham gave a small, impatient growl. "Cut the crap, Rafe. I can smell her all over you. If you want to keep lying to yourself, fine; it's no fur off my hide. But you're an idiot if you think you can keep lying to yourself."

"What do you mean, you can smell her? I haven't seen Tess in hours. You should be able to smell nothing."

"Tell that to the pheromones that are clinging to you like dry burrs. It smells like *she's* the one with the Feline tendencies, and that she spent the last four or five hours stropping up against you like her own personal scratching post. If you two were Lupine, I'd say you'd already marked her."

Lupines staked a permanent physical claim on their mates by biting them during sex. The mark gave visual proof of the partnership as well as leaving an indelible scent mark to warn others that this particular person had been taken out of the potential mating pool. Some Felines had a similar tradition, but it wasn't one Rafe had ever performed. In fact, he'd never even considered it.

Of course, until he'd met Tess, he'd never considered he might meet a woman he couldn't get out of his head.

"But we are not, and I have done nothing of the kind," he snapped, throwing a few bills down on their table and grabbing his coat from the empty chair beside him. "Your nose must be mistaken."

Graham followed him out of the restaurant and had to stretch his long legs to keep pace with his friend's angry strides. "Hey, don't shoot the messenger, all right? I'm just saying what I think. If that's pissing you off, I guess I'll keep my mouth shut. Happy?"

"Ecstatic."

The baring of his teeth somewhat blunted the effect of his response, but Graham had finally seemed to take the hint that this wasn't a subject Rafe wanted to discuss, and he fell silent.

Hell, it wasn't even a topic Rafe wanted to think about, but now he couldn't seem to think about anything else. What the hell had happened to him over the course of that last week, and where had it left him?

The answer to the first part of the question came

to him in a single syllable: *Tess*. Tess had happened to him.

She had popped into his life like the clown out of a jack-in-the-box, completely unexpected and, frankly, a little bit frightening. To be honest, it would have been much easier for him if his stalker that night had turned out to be a hired assassin. That sort of threat he could have neutralized and moved on from without even a second glance. He'd dealt with similar in the past, and he'd always managed to come out on top. A threat to his life didn't scare him, but the threat Tess Menzies represented to his heart had him terrified out of his wits.

What man in his right mind would not be frightened of the prospect of his entire life turning upside down? Tess represented just that sort of monumental shift to his reality. Before meeting her, he had known what his future would hold. He would continue to make his merry way through the world as he had always done. He had plenty of wealth to make his life comfortable and a number of close friends to keep him entertained. His work—both in the world of business and in the world of the Others—kept him engaged and challenged, and he had never found any difficulty in acquiring a female companion to satisfy his more basic needs. There had been no reason why he could not have continued indefinitely in such a manner. Of course, at some point he would have liked to find a female with whom he might sire a cub so that he could rest easy in the knowledge that his mark in the world would live on after his own death. He was a man, after all, and a proud man at that, and most men wanted sons.

Now that he had met Tess, though, his wants seemed destined to take a backseat to his needs.

He needed her.

He almost winced at the thought. Rafael De Santos was not the sort of man accustomed to needing anyone. Like the jungle beast that lived inside him, Rafe considered himself independent by nature, the sort of man who preferred to live, to hunt, to be alone. Crowds often made him uneasy, the press of bodies making him want to snarl and snap and slink away to somewhere still and quiet. He enjoyed the company of his friends, people like Graham and Dmitri and, these days, even their ever-growing circle of spouses, mates, and acquaintances. He appreciated lively conversation and enjoyed the opportunity to laugh with those whom he respected and understood. All of that felt natural to him and fit neatly into the world he had already made for himself.

Nowhere in that world had he envisioned making room for a mate.

It went beyond his isolationist nature, however. Part of the reason Rafe had never envisioned choosing a mate had lingered in the back of his mind since his earliest childhood. He had never spared it much thought, never brooded over it or questioned it; it had simply always lurked in the background, like a dark mist obscuring corners he hadn't cared all that much about exploring. Why worry, after all, over something he could never change?

Why think about the curse?

He had told Graham he didn't believe in the legend, that it was nothing more than an old wives' tale. Who believed in things like curses and legacies and the actions of a distant ancestor reverberating down through the ages anymore? It made no logical sense to imagine that there had ever been a witch who fell in love with a jaguar, or that, having been spurned by a faithless cat, she would remove the ability of his entire species to thrive and multiply. Was such a thing even possible? Rafe had never believed so. He had never believed that the actions of some kind of great-great-great-great-grandfather were the reason why his kind never bothered to find mates. Jaguar cats never took permanent mates, so why should the shifters who shared their forms?

But then, it was hard to ignore certain facts. Cat species had never been known for their fidelity to the opposite sex, but they also rarely had trouble conceiving or bearing young. In the wild, jaguars mated and then went their separate ways, but four months later the female would give birth to a litter of cubs. In the animal kingdom, after all, fidelity had never been a requirement for reproduction.

The same was true of all the spotted cats, from leopards to cheetahs to lynxes and ocelots. In the wild, mating resulted in kits more often than not, but in their shifter counterparts, conception had become a hard-fought struggle. In modern times, only one in every fifty female spotted-cat shifters would conceive. Most never bothered with birth control because the chances of accidental pregnancy were so small. The females also tended to conceive later in life— after thirty-five was not uncommon—because it took years of concentrated effort to achieve a pregnancy. The least optimistic among his kind predicted that spotted-cat shifters would die out within the next two to three hundred years. The most superstitious blamed those problems on the curse, but Rafe had never been a superstitious man.

Hell, he barely believed in Fate. He supposed he had accepted in a sort of general way that there might be some kind of higher power at work in the lives of those on earth. When he thought about life and death, about wars and rescues, about natural disasters and people who survived extraordinary events, that kind of idea made sense. What he wasn't certain he believed was the idea that every man and woman had a mate they were destined to be with. For pity's sake, he barely believed in fidelity, and he was supposed to believe in love?

Because he had to face it: Love beat like a heart at the center of everything. Love had created the curse after it had been betrayed and cast aside; love was the reason shifters took mates, the reason why Dmitri had turned Regina and Graham had marked Missy. Love was even what Graham alluded to when he talked about the way Rafe seemed unable to keep his mind off Tess—but could love really be what he felt for his maddening little witch?

He liked her with no question. He liked her spunky attitude and her sharp tongue, her tendency toward grumpiness and her oddball sense of humor. He especially liked the way she felt against him, and over him and beneath him, but what did that really mean? That he should take her to mate? What would be the point? He was a Feline; eventually, he would grow restless and drift away, the way his kind always did, and Tess would be left behind with a bunch of broken promises just as the witch in the legend had been. If he never made promises, wouldn't that be better? Wouldn't she rather not have that betrayal on top of all the rest when she was free to move on to other relationships? To men who would be able to stay beyond that first flush of passion.

Men who wouldn't be Rafe.

"Hey, you all right?"

Rafe jerked his attention back to the present and caught Graham's frown of concern. He must have snarled out loud.

The thought of another man putting his hands on Tess dropped a red curtain of rage across Rafe's field of vision. Every cell in his body roared in outrage at the idea of any man but him seeing her creamy curves, touching her soft skin, tasting her rich, intoxicating flavors. His heartbeat thudded fast and loud in his ears and his breathing grew sharp and shallow. He felt his skin tingle and crawl the way it did before a shift, and his animal fought with claw and fang for the freedom to hunt and kill the rival threat.

Christ. He had to get ahold of himself.

"Rafe."

Graham halted in the middle of the sidewalk and reached out a hand. Rafe batted it away with a rumble of warning.

"Do not touch me," he gritted out, stepping to the side to lean against the wall of the adjacent building. He closed his eyes and fought hard against the beast within him. "Just give me a moment. I will be fine. A moment."

He felt the wolf's shadow pass over him as Graham positioned himself at his side. Even that seemed like a challenge to his furious inner jaguar. Graham might be one of Rafe's closest friends, but all his beast knew was that the wolf was a mature, Alpha male, and it wanted to kill the potential rival for his witchy mate.

What the hell was happening to him?

Rafe concentrated on the feel of the concrete at his back, the warmth of the sun on his face, and the monotonous drone of pedestrians and car traffic that filled the air around him.

Deep breaths. Out and in. Out with tension. In with relaxation.

In.

And out.

"Uh, don't take this the wrong way, buddy," Graham hissed, his voice dully penetrating Rafe's intense concentration, "but get a fucking hold of yourself. It's two in the afternoon and you're standing on the corner of Lex and Eighty-Seventh *growing fur*. What the hell is wrong with you?"

Rafe's eyes flew open, and he followed Graham's glare down to his own hands. Hand that currently sported long, black claws and a light, dense coating of golden fur punctuated with irregular black spots.

Fuck.

Hastily, he shoved his hands into the pockets of his coat and ducked his head into his chest.

"What else?" he growled, wincing when he heard his own voice. It had gone low and gravelly, sounding more animal than human, and feral at that.

"Your eyes have changed completely," Graham murmured, turning him toward the less crowded cross-street and urging him forward. The Lupine set a brisk pace back toward Vircolac. "A cabbie would have a heart attack the minute he caught sight of you. Your nose is also flattened, and I can see your facial markings bleeding into your skin. You're goddamned out of control."

Graham was right, and Rafe knew it. Damn it, this was what that witch did to him. She stripped away his control and turned him into an animal for the whole world to see.

And if any of the world noticed, Rafe would find himself in a steel cage being dissected while the rest of the Other world tried to deal with the collateral damage of a very unexpected and abrupt Unveiling.

"Keep your head down, and for God's sake get a grip, furrball." Graham snagged a fedora from the sidewalk display of a tiny shop with one hand and tossed cash at the protesting vendor with the other. Hurriedly, he crammed it on his friend's head and lengthened their strides even further.

Rafe obeyed the first command and struggled with the second. At least the fear of imminent discovery was serving to distract him somewhat from thoughts of Tess. Or more specifically from thoughts of Tess with another man.

A roar of challenge caught in his throat, and Rafe cursed silently. He hadn't had this much trouble controlling his beast since puberty, damn it. He should be able to do this.

Risking a quick tilt of his head, Rafe turned his gaze toward the sign on the corner and realized they had reached the street that housed the club. Thank God. Just a few more yards, and they could get inside where it would be safe. Then Rafe could beat himself into unconsciousness if that was what it took to put his jaguar back to sleep.

At this point, he feared that might be necessary.

The only bright spot at the moment was that at least Tess wasn't around to see this. First, he couldn't guarantee his jaguar wouldn't leap right on top of her, take her neck in its jaws, and carry her away to its lair for a rough and thorough claiming. But even more than that, he didn't quite feel comfortable with the idea of her seeing him like this, so out of control.

Even if it was all her fault.

Fifteen

Graham hustled Rafe up the steps and into the club as if the sidewalk were on fire. Not that Rafe felt inclined to protest. Out of sight would hopefully be out of mind for any human passersby who might have gotten a glimpse of his partially shifted features. If they were very lucky, the traditional human coping mechanism would come into play and any observers would find themselves remembering not a half-human half-jaguar man practically jogging through the streets of the city, but a man in strange pre-Halloween makeup, or someone with an unsightly skin disease at whom it would be impolite to stare. Usually, humans came up with some sort of explanation for any Others they sighted that involved nothing remotely supernatural, and that was exactly the way the Council of Others hoped to keep it. At least for the moment.

As soon as they stepped into the club's entry hall, Graham turned them away from the areas frequented by the members and straight into his private offices. Rafe felt grateful for that. Having a human see him in his current condition would prove disastrous for the secrecy of the Others; having an Other see him this way would prove disastrous for his reputation and for his authority as head of the Council. The inability of a shifter to control his change counted as a sign of weakness, and Rafe couldn't afford to appear weak, especially not in the current uneasy climate. Everyone knew the Unveiling was coming, but it would take a strong leader to take the community smoothly through the transition. A leader perceived as weak could never hold them together.

Graham shut the office door behind them and leaned against it for a moment, looking exhausted. Rafe couldn't blame him. He felt pretty tired himself, mostly from struggling against his shift. Now, though, in the calm of the quietly furnished room, he could feel some of the tension beginning to drain from him. Reaching up, he removed the hat Graham had pressed on him and ran his fingers through his hair.

"Any better?"

"Better than what?"

The female voice made both him and Graham turn toward the large desk that blocked the door to Graham's inner sanctum from the outer office. Rafe hadn't even thought about Samantha, Graham's assistant, who occupied her usual spot in front of her computer.

"Long story," Graham muttered, raking his gaze

over his friend's face. "Some, but not completely normal. And I have to say, you're freaking me out with this. Frankly, I think I need a damned drink."

Pushing away from the door, Graham stalked toward his inner sanctuary, jerking his head for Rafe to follow.

"Hey, wait," Sam called, jumping from her seat and moving to block the entry. "You can't go in there."

The brunette Lupine might be strong and toned, but she presented no sort of threat to her pack Alpha and very little to Rafe, whose jaguar form outweighed even her wolf by at least a hundred pounds. She didn't appear to consider that, though, as she tried to prevent the men from moving into the inner office. She at least had the good sense to do it while keeping her eyes cast toward the floor, thereby making it clear she had no intention of actually challenging her Alpha.

Nevertheless, Graham didn't appear to be in the mood to wait out here by Sam's desk. He growled and reached out, grasping the woman by the shoulders and physically moving her out of his way.

"Not now, Sam. It's already been a long day, and it isn't even three o'clock. Tell anyone who stops by that I'm not in, and hold all my calls. I'll return messages later."

He spoke over his shoulder, so he was turned away from his office door even as he swung the panel open and stepped forward. It was Rafe's muttered curse that made his attention snap back to the inner office and the visitor who waited inside.

A visitor named Lionel Menzies.

Rafe might have asked Graham to dig into Menzies's background, but he'd also taken a few minutes of his own time to do a quick Internet search on Tess's grandfather. Apparently, the banker played a prominent enough part in Manhattan society that his photo appeared regularly in the papers and on the websites of various industry and charitable organizations. Rafe recognized him immediately.

Tall and thin, with pale, wrinkled skin and sharp blue eyes, Lionel Menzies possessed a military bearing and a sour expression. He stood with his back toward Graham's desk, facing the door, with his hands clasped behind his back and his feet spread at shoulder width. His shoulders had begun to curl with age, but he still managed to stand so that he appeared firmly upright and confident. Rafe thought the illusion might be strengthened by the height he achieved with his nose held so high in the air.

His blue eyes appeared a bare shade lighter than his granddaughter's, but they lacked even a fraction of her warmth. They passed over Graham and locked on Rafe, narrowing with icy indignation.

"So *this* is the man the Council of Others has chosen to lead them? A shifter so weak he can't even contain his own beast? Is this some sort of joke?"

Samantha cleared her throat behind them, and Graham and Rafe turned their heads to see her shrug apologetically. "I tried to warn you. He didn't have an appointment, but he wouldn't let me brush him off. He insisted on waiting for you. He's been here for nearly an hour."

Having witnessed Samantha at work before and having seen her deal with drunken vampires, lust-crazed weres, and terrified swanmay, Rafe knew Lionel Menzies had to be one stubborn son of a bitch to have withstood the Lupine's efforts to be rid of him. Of course, knowing Tess, that didn't come as a huge shock. She had to have inherited her determination from someone.

The unexpected confrontation with his lover's grandfather and a powerful force behind the desire of the Witches' Council to meet with him accomplished what Rafe had been struggling with for the past twenty minutes. He felt his beast settle back in its lair with a disgruntled rumble and felt his features settle back in their normal—human—lines. Drawing his hands from his pockets, he stepped forward and offered one to the scowling witch.

"Mr. Menzies," he said in his smoothest, most professional head-of-the-Council voice, "I am Rafael De Santos. It is a pleasure to make your acquaintance. I apologize that neither Graham nor I was here to greet you. Would you care to sit down before we talk?"

The witch ignored his outstretched hand—or to be

honest, he spared it a disgusted glance before tugging at the cuff of his expensively cut suit coat and stepping around the Others toward the exit.

"I would *not* care to sit," Lionel bit out, "and as far as I am concerned, we have nothing to talk about. Now please step aside."

"Wait a minute," Graham growled, glaring at his unexpected guest. "I'm not sure how things operate among you magic users, but around here you don't force your way into a man's office and then refuse to shake the hand of his friend. And you especially don't storm out without so much as an explanation of what you wanted in the first place. So why don't you tell us what you came here for, old man, before I decide not to bother with my own good manners."

Rafe winced. This was why Graham was never meant to head the Council of Others. The Lupine wouldn't recognize diplomacy if it sat beside him and howled at the moon. Before Rafe could open his mouth, though, Lionel had already fired back.

"Where I come from, *boy,*" the elderly man sneered, "a man is not expected to shake hands with an animal. And whatever I came here for became irrelevant the moment I realized that the individual my colleagues intended to rely on as a rational voice for the Other community is little better than a rabid beast. I had hoped to have an intelligent, preliminary discussion of the ways in which our communities could cooperate to ensure the continuation and even strengthening of our vital Accord, but I can see now that such an endeavor would be not only fruit-less, but ridiculous. Clearly if your kind is willing to walk the streets in daylight where any human can see you looking like animal freaks, the only choice my brethren and I have is to decide when we can ex-pect a return to the hostilities the Accord was drafted to stop. From what I've seen here, it's clear to me that the answer will be almost immediately."

With that, the old man shouldered his way past the shifters and out the office door, slamming it behind him. A second later, they heard the muffled slam of the club's main door as well. Menzies had apparently blown off Vircolac's butler in addition to its owner.

With a sigh, Rafe released Graham's arm where he'd grabbed his friend to prevent him from taking a swing at the angry witch. Rafe might have felt an equal desire to maim the rude old bigot, but he real-ized that physical violence would solve nothing. In fact, it would only have confirmed Menzies's obvi-ous assumption that shapeshifters were little better than the animals whose forms they took.

"Wow. Well, isn't he the charmer?" Sam quipped, stepping into the office and pulling a bottle and a couple of glasses from a cabinet. "To what did we owe that pleasure, boss?"

She handed each of the men a liberal dose of whiskey and grabbed a third glass for herself.

"Normally, I don't drink on the job," she said to Rafe, "but damned if that old bastard hasn't given me a reason to start."

Graham tossed back his drink with one swallow. "*Old bastard* is right. Was that son of a bitch really your Tess's grandfather?"

" 'His Tess'?" Sam echoed, eyebrows rising.

"She is not my Tess," Rafe growled, even as his jaguar roared that she damned well was. He didn't have time to deal with that at the moment. "But yes, that was him. I am surprised that a man with his manners lasted as their council's High Authority for so many years. I would have thought a temper such as his would not lend itself to such a sensitive position."

"Right. So what the hell did he want?" Graham snatched the whiskey bottle from Sam and refilled both their glasses. Rafe had yet to touch his drink.

Rafe shrugged. "You know as much as I do, my friend. According to his little speech, he had intended to speak with us in advance of my scheduled meeting with the Witches' Council."

Sam's eyes widened. "You have a meeting with the witches? Seriously? When did that happen? I thought those guys kept to themselves more than cult-following mountain people. Why do they suddenly want to meet with us?"

"Cut the crap," Graham said, shooting her a quelling glance. "We all know you've already gotten the scoop from Melissa. You probably know as much about the meeting as I do and even more about Tess."

"Tessa Bryony Menzies. Twenty-nine. Blond hair, blue eyes, hootchie mama figure." Sam grinned and set her glass down with a click. "Owns an herb-and-tea shop in the East Village and demonstrates an impressive ability to read tarot cards. Only child of Geoffrey and Roberta Menzies, both deceased. Currently single, but there *is* a certain amount of speculation in some quarters as to how long that might last."

With that, she turned her gaze on Rafe and wriggled her eyebrows.

He growled. "Tess is none of your business, and the meeting with the Witches' Council was supposed to take place on the night of the next full moon. Now, however, I am not even sure if such a meeting will take place."

"Why wouldn't it?" Graham asked. "Their council members were the ones to request it. Do you really think they would cancel just because one ex-member got bent out of shape when he spotted your spots?"

"I don't know," Rafe admitted. "I am still not sure if I know what the meeting was for in the first place."

"Um, didn't he just tell you that?" Sam questioned. "I mean, he yelled it so loud that I'm sure half the club could answer that question. It had to do with the Accord, which I'm assuming refers to the Accord of Silence, and not an imported and best-selling Japanese sedan."

"So we were led to believe. I am just unsure as to why the topic would come up now. It has been well over three hundred years since the Accord went into effect, yet the witches choose now to make the first contact with the Others in all that time?"

"I have been wondering about that," Graham said. "Misha, too. I mean, everyone on the Council—hell, everyone who's been paying the slightest bit of attention—knows that we won't be able to put off the Unveiling all that much longer. Another couple of years, maybe. But it's a lot easier for the witches to blend in with the humans. What would make them so nervous now that they feel the need to reinforce an agreement that's worked perfectly well for literally centuries?"

Rafe shook his head. "I have been unable to puzzle it out. I had hoped the meeting would answer those questions, but now I am left questioning whether the meeting will even occur."

"Have you considered asking Tess about that?"

Rafe explained to Sam, "Tess's grandfather does not respect her or her abilities. He has not shared any information about the meeting with her. She remains nearly as in the dark as we are."

"Couldn't she find out, though?" Sam pressed. "I mean, it sucks to be underestimated, especially by family, but sometimes it can actually be an advantage. People tend to be pretty talkative around people they don't think have a stake in their plans. Maybe she could overhear something if she put herself in the right place at the right time."

"You mean we should have her spy on the old bastard," Graham snorted.

"To-may-to, to-mah-to."

"No," Rafe said. "I could never ask Tess to put herself into a position that caused trouble with her family. The man is her grandfather."

"Her grandfather who thinks she's an idiot and treats her like a lackey, from what Missy says. Frankly, it doesn't sound like they have much of a relationship to damage."

Graham shot Rafe a look. "She could at least find out whether they intend to go ahead with the meeting. That should be fairly easy for her to find out, don't you think?"

Rafe hesitated. Tess had mentioned to him that she was expected to appear at Lionel's house every Sunday evening for dinner. In fact, this past Sunday had been one of the nights when he had been forced to summon all his patience and not let himself into her apartment until close to midnight. She always needed time alone, she had told him, to decompress from her family dining ordeal. Sunday came again in two days.

"I can ask her after she returns if her grandfather mentions anything," he grudgingly agreed, "but I cannot ask that she spy or that she try to obtain detailed information. He is her family, after all."

"Hey, a little info is better than none," Sam said and offered him a reassuring smile. "But try not to worry. From what I hear, Tess sounds like the kind of girl who can look out for herself."

Sixteen

"East Village Apothecary. This is Tess. How can I help you?"

"Are you pregnant?"

Tess dropped a three-hundred-dollar bag of saffron on her foot. Luckily, it weighed less than a pound.

"What!" she screeched.

"Are you pregnant?" Missy's voice sounded breathless and very excited. Even the phone lines couldn't hide it. "I know it's a weird way to start a conversation, and I'll get to the hellos and how-are-yous later. First, I need to know if you're pregnant."

"What the hell kind of question is that?" She scooped up the bag—which had thankfully remained tightly sealed—and stuffed it back under the counter. She could divide it up later. When her heart stopped beating three hundred times a minute.

"The kind you need to answer. Just tell me, Tess. Pregnant. Yes, or no."

Her denial was instant, vehement, and totally unfounded. "Of course not."

She hadn't even considered the possibility. Because it was impossible. Ridiculous. Laughable.

Terrifying.

"Why would you even ask me something like that?" she demanded.

"Aside from the fact that you and Rafe have been screwing like rabid bunnies for seven and three-quarters of the last eight days?"

"For God's sake, Missy! You don't have to shout it." She looked around at the Friday-afternoon browsers in the shop as if she thought some of them might have overheard the other half of the conversation she was conducting on the cordless phone. Hell, Missy was yelling so loud, some of them might have. They all continued to shop, though, and she turned her back, heading for the small, semi-private alcove where she usually did her tarot readings. Not that she'd done any since the one with Missy.

"Even if such a thing were remotely possible—which it isn't—"

Please, God!

"—how the hell would I know? You said yourself, it's only been eight days. It would take fourteen, minimum, before I even had time to skip a . . . period." She hesitated and lowered her voice before that last bit. Bette was already eyeing her too warily from behind the lavender stalks.

"When you're knocked up by a shapeshifter, you know. Come over. Now."

"Now? Missy, I can't just up and leave work in the middle of—"

"Now."

"Missy, tonight is—"

"Now."

Wow. Tess hadn't realized the other woman could growl like that. She must have been taking lessons from her husband.

"Fine," Tess said. "I'll see if Bette minds closing for me. If it's okay with her, I can leave in an hour, right after I—"

"Now."

"All right! Sheesh. Give me thirty minutes—"

"Now."

"It will take me at least fifteen, even if I hijack the first cab on the avenue."

"Fine. But leave *now*!"

Seventeen minutes and forty-three seconds later, Tess shoved her fare into the cabbie's hand and leaped out of the taxi. Another three seconds later, she was pounding on the Winterses' door and wondering if maybe she needed to see someone about her blood pressure.

Missy jerked the door open before the echo of the first knock faded and hauled Tess inside by the front of her shirt.

"Holy shit, Missy! What the hell do you do in your spare time? Bench press Volvos?"

The blond woman ignored her. She was too busy sticking her nose up against Tess's neck and inhaling deeply.

"What the hell . . . ?"

Missy pulled back, her eyes wide. She blinked up at Tess. "I don't get it. You're not pregnant."

Tess threw up her hands and contemplated joining a remote Buddhist monastery in Tibet. Someplace where everyone took vows of silence. And no sniffing. "I know I'm not pregnant. In fact, I tried to tell you so over the phone. So what gives?"

Missy just shook her head and turned, heading toward the same sitting room Tess had visited unwillingly last Wednesday night. "I really don't get it. You have to be pregnant. There's no other explanation."

Torn between offering to call Missy a doctor and trying to wring her neck, Tess gave an exasperated cry and chased after her.

"What don't you get?" she demanded. "That I'm not pregnant? I hate to burst your bubble, but there's a very good explanation for that. It's called wild carrot seed. I've been taking the tincture since the first time your friend laid his grubby little paws on me!"

Missy stopped at the entrance to the living room and whirled around, one hand on her hip, the other curled around the shining brass doorknob. "That still," she growled, "doesn't explain this!"

With impeccable timing, perfectly synchronized to her shout, Missy turned her hand and threw open the door to reveal three very confused-looking women. Who otherwise appeared completely normal.

Tess blinked. "Um, oooookay. What do they have to do with anything? And who are they?"

"They"—Missy stabbed a finger through the door-way—"are all pregnant. Just like you should be."

"Huh?"

"Every single one of those women has gotten knocked up—in the past week—by a werecat of the spotted variety."

Tess's head snapped around, searching for the near-est butcher's knife. "You mean to tell me that Rafe—"

"No! Of course not. I didn't mean Rafe person-ally got all these women pregnant."

Tess watched the red haze recede.

"The fact that they're all pregnant is definitely your fault."

"Missy, I'm not sure how different the reproduc-tive biologies of the shapeshifting species are, but I only know of a limited number of ways to get preg-nant, and they all involve at least two sexes."

"Stop being such a moron. I wasn't speaking bio-logically. I was speaking mystically. Magically. You know, like the stuff curses are made of."

Tess jerked back as if she'd just been stabbed with a hot poker. She almost wanted to check for singe-ing. "Whoa. Curse? As in Rafe's curse? The one you ambushed me with last week?"

"It wasn't an ambush. It was a strategic covert op-eration."

"What are you? The press secretary for the Joint Chiefs of Staff?"

"That's not the point. The point is that these three women are pregnant today because of you."

Tess winced. "I really wish you'd stop saying it like that before one of them decides to sue me for child support."

"Oh, we wouldn't do that," a tall, leggy blonde said in a breathless Marilyn Monroe voice. "We didn't even know you existed until the Luna said something. We just came to report the upcoming births to the Felix. That's what we're supposed to do, isn't it?"

Missy nodded at her, leading her to the sofa and urging her to sit. "You did just fine, Fawn. Everything is fine. Just sit here until Tess and I finish talking."

Tess tugged Missy back out into the hallway and looked into the living room with suspicious eyes. "Does carrying a shifter's baby suck brain cells, or has she always been like that?"

"No, that's just Fawn. We think she got her name because she's about as smart as one. But do you see what I mean?"

"About what?"

"About it being your fault?"

"Missy! No, I do not see what you mean. I don't even see what language you're speaking." She realized she was shouting and lowered her voice. "I am so beyond confused that I don't even think I could find my way back with a map. Why does it matter that these three women are going to have kittens?"

"Didn't you listen to anything we told you last week? Spotted Felines don't just get women pregnant. It doesn't work that way."

"Actually, what you told me was that the birthrate was declining. Clearly it's not dead yet, or the whole race would be extinct."

Missy growled in exasperation. She sounded a lot like Graham. "Yeah, but it's been declining for hundreds and hundreds of years. Last year there were seven spotted Feline births in New York. Seven! All year. And now we have three pregnancies in one week? What does that say to you?"

"Nothing!" Tess threw up her hands. "It says nothing to me, because I have no idea what you're getting at! Last week you told me about a curse on the spotted Feline shifters that said pregnancy couldn't happen until a Felix stayed faithful to a witch for a year and a day. Rafe has only been with me for eight bloody days! And even if I *have* kept him too busy to sleep with anyone else, that's still not enough time to undo your bloody curse! So what the hell are you trying to tell me?"

The blond woman took a deep breath and spoke again, slower and more softly this time. "I'm trying to tell you that maybe the legend is wrong. Maybe the year-and-a-day thing isn't really necessary. Maybe once *you* get pregnant, anyone can get pregnant. Or maybe Rafe only needs to fall in love with you to lift the curse. I'm not sure. But I am sure that you have something to do with the answer, and that's why I dragged you all the way across town."

"Missy, I can't—"

"Just listen. I have a theory."

"Miss—"

"Listen." The Luna took a deep breath and began pacing. "I was thinking about it after lunch, while I was nursing Roark. See, until he's weaned, I still have some Lupine abilities. Not like I did while I was pregnant, and not like a real Lupine, of course, but echoes of the things they can do. I love it. I'll be sorry to stop nursing, because I know that's when it will really fade away. See, at the moment, I have the most amazing connection to Graham. I can see things the way he does. I can smell them. It's like looking at the world through Lupine eyes. I mean, I know he still sees and smells and tastes things so much more clearly than me, but I'm only human. At least I get to see the echoes. And I got to thinking about that. About echoes, and the connection that forms between a shifter and a non-shifter when she's carrying his child."

Tess sighed impatiently, but she listened.

"And I started to think maybe that was the secret to the curse," Missy continued. "What if it wasn't about being faithful to a non-Feline for a year and a day, but about having that connection to one. I figured, what if all the witch wanted was for a Felix to experience that connection to a non-Feline, to become almost like the same person for the time that the witch he mated with was pregnant. That's why I called to ask if you were pregnant. I thought you must be, if it had managed to lift the curse."

"Well, I hate to disappoint you, but I'm not." Tess made a face. "Look, I know you're only trying to help the Felines, and I do understand, Missy, but I just don't have time for this right now. The last week of my life has been utter chaos. I've missed more hours of work in these past few days than in the last seven years combined. I have orders backing up from here to kingdom come, and if I ask Bette to cover for me one more time, I think she's going to cover me with wet cement before throwing me into the East River. I have to go."

Missy sighed. "I know. I just got so excited when I thought I'd figured it out."

Tess reached out and hugged the other woman impulsively. "I know, and I appreciate it. And as soon as this business with the councils meeting is over, we'll figure it out together, okay?"

Missy hugged her back. "If you say so. But I honestly thought I had it. I mean, if all these Feline pregnancies didn't happen because Rafe knocked you up, what the heck is going on here?"

Seventeen

Tess stepped out of the subway station still mumbling over Missy's question. As if she had *any idea* what the heck was going on in her life these days. The last clue she'd possessed had gotten knocked clean out of her the minute Rafe tackled her in the alley on Wednesday night. Since then, she'd barely been able to tell if she was coming or going.

Except mostly, she'd been coming.

Rafe seemed unable to keep his hands off her, which was flattering, she acknowledged, but also a little freaky. Tess knew she was cute, knew men responded to her blond curls and her blue eyes and her curvy figure, but they didn't usually insinuate themselves quite so far into her life within the first ten days of the relationship. Though to be accurate, it had actually been only nine days; so, you know, one day freakier.

Her alley cat encounter had happened on Wednesday night. By Saturday, he had managed somehow—she still wasn't quite sure how it had happened—to wheedle a spare key from her so that even when she retained enough sense not to let him take her back to his place, she still couldn't stay away from him. Or rather, Rafe couldn't stay away from her. If she didn't present herself in his apartment by ten o'clock each night, he magically appeared at hers. Usually hungry.

Not that Tess could complain about the sex, mind you, unless she intended to complain about getting too much of it, and she just didn't have that kinda crazy. Sex with the werecat continued to burn hot enough to sear the sheets and intense enough that she'd given up any pretense of working out at a gym because her heart rate got up into the cardiac fitness zone every time Rafe so much as laid a hand on her. The intensity of the chemistry between them frankly overwhelmed her.

In fact, that word summed up Tess's entire life at the moment: *overwhelming.*

Stuffing her hands into her pockets, she trudged around the corner, deep in thought. Missy's chosen topic for the afternoon hadn't exactly done much to reassure her, either. Pregnancy just wasn't the kind of thing Tess left up to chance. If she ever had kids— and she kind of hoped she would someday—she did not intend to bring them into the world as a single mom. Heck, it was hard enough to take care of herself as a working professional; add kids to the mix, and she could envision nothing but trouble. No, children didn't figure in to her life plan until *after* she had met Mr. Right and heard him utter those three little words:

I am committed. The tincture of wild carrot she took daily was just her little insurance policy.

Missy had seemed surprised that Tess had thought about birth control since meeting Rafe. Granted, lust-induced stupidity had swept the thought from her mind during their first encounter, but one of the first things she'd done the next day was take her tincture. Thankfully, the stuff was effective as a plan B option, but she sure hadn't missed a dose since then. Rafe might still be sniffing at her door more than a week after their meeting, but who knew how long that behavior would last? In Tess's experience, men couldn't exactly be called the most faithful bunch on the planet, and from what she'd gathered from Missy and her friends, Feline men sounded even less inclined to settle in for the long haul. Without that kind of commitment, Tess considered her womb closed for business.

Unfortunately, all that logic didn't seem to be doing her much good in taking her mind off what intentions Rafe might actually have toward her. Sure, he reached for her each time with just as much enthusiasm as he had from the first, but after just nine days, what did that really mean?

"Most likely? That even cats are horny pigs," she muttered to herself as she skirted a car that had managed to park with its front passenger tire all the way up on the curb. Some people just shouldn't be allowed to own cars in Manhattan.

Narrowly resisting the urge to take her frustration and sour mood out on the unsuspecting vehicle, she pressed close against the stairs of the adjacent building and picked her way through the narrow slice of open sidewalk.

The premonition hit her three seconds before the first blow did.

In her mind's eye, she saw the pipe swing down, aiming for the back of her head. She also saw the split in her scalp, the dark spray of blood, black in the poorly lit space between streetlamps, and the depressed fracture at the back of her skull. She saw herself fall and saw the glassy blankness of her own eyes staring sightlessly up at the night sky. She saw all of it in a fraction of a second, and in the next fraction, she twisted, raising her arms to shield the back of her head and screaming bloody murder, because that was exactly what her attacker had intended.

Instead of connecting with the back of Tess's skull, her attacker's aim was thrown off the mark by her sudden and unexpected movement. The intended killing blow glanced off her shoulder and back, still packing enough force to send pain exploding through her senses. She screamed again and heard a man's voice cursing in the shadows. A stray beam of light glinted off dull metal as he raised the pipe for a second blow.

The third scream was the charm.

Tess spun and jumped onto the stairs, and the second strike caught her across the upper thigh. It felt like she imagined thunder would feel, if it could hit a person instead of just deafening them, and it sent her tumbling onto her ass. She saw stars—literally—but the pain took her breath away, so she could hear an angry shout and the sound of running footsteps pounding in her direction.

Her attacker, heavily camouflaged in a hooded jacket and dark bandanna, swore again and took off running, leaving Tess struggling to breathe and wishing for morphine.

"Holy shit!" someone said, the voice female but surprisingly powerful. Tess supposed it had to be in order to frighten off an armed mugger. "Did he get you? Are you hurt?"

"Yes, and I think so, but not badly."

Tess winced and raised her spinning head to thank the woman who had probably saved her life. Part of her had expected to see a policewoman, or maybe a female wrestler—someone either well armed or bulging with muscles. Instead, she saw a tall, slim African American woman with coffee-colored skin, dark eyes, and hair so black that it glinted blue when she passed under the streetlights.

"You're lucky, then," the woman told her, stopping at the base of the steps Tess sat on and bracing her hands on her hips. "He looked like he was trying to kill you."

"That's only because he was."

Tess winced and used the railing to lever herself to her feet. Her hands still shook from the aftermath of her adrenaline surge, her shoulder and back screamed like they were on fire, and her thigh barely wanted to support her weight. And still she knew she had gotten off lightly. If her magic hadn't warned her of the coming attack, she could very well be dead right now.

"I should thank you," she said, trying to muster a smile even as she cradled her right arm close against her body to lessen the strain on her injury. "He was about to come at me again when we heard you approaching. If you hadn't come along, he could have killed me."

The stranger's eyes narrowed. "Well, I'm damned glad to see you're alive, because I have a bone to pick with you, and it would be a hell of a lot less satisfying for me if I'd had to resort to telling off your corpse."

Tess blinked. "Excuse me?"

"Not that I wouldn't have done it," the woman continued. Tess's position standing on the second stair of the building entry put them eye-to-eye, and she could see that her erstwhile rescuer looked plenty mad. "In fact, I'm so ticked off right now, I can't guarantee I wouldn't have kicked you when you were down. You've got a hell of a lot of nerve, lady!"

Right, because Tess hadn't been feeling confused enough before this.

"Um, look," she began, eyeing the strange woman warily, "I'm really grateful for your help and everything, but I have no idea who you are or what the hell you're talking about, so I'm just going to be on my way now, all right? You have a good night."

The woman didn't touch Tess, but she stepped to

the side to block the way and keep Tess on the steps. With her brown eyes blazing and her lips pressed in a narrow line, the stranger looked a lot like an angry girlfriend, only Tess felt pretty sure she would have remembered if she'd ever dated a woman, let alone pissed one off enough for an angry public scene.

"I'll tell you what I'm talking about," the woman growled, "and you're damned well going to listen. My name is Anisia Cuma, and it seems we didn't need to meet before now for you to completely screw up my life."

"Okay, are you looking for directions to Bellevue? Because I'm not sure—"

Anisia growled again, this time sounding an awful lot like Rafe did when Tess told him they really needed to spend some time apart from each other, or at least not in bed with each other. "I'm not crazy, lady; I'm pregnant. And it's all your frickin' fault."

Oh, for the sake of everything holy!

Tess sighed and pushed her way around the other woman, gasping through her teeth when the move jostled her shoulder and sent white-hot arrows of pain shooting through her. She so wasn't in the mood for this conversation, especially not if it was headed in the direction she feared.

And that had nothing to do with a premonition. It was just that after everything that had happened today, only something this horrifying could possibly top it all off.

"Let me guess," she grumbled, setting off down

the street at a brisk hobble. "You must be Feline—spotted Feline, I'm guessing—and despite the fact that we're living in the twenty-first century and you look like the kind of girl who got at least an elementary education, you've gotten it into your head that you're pregnant because of the lifting of some ridiculous curse that probably never existed. Am I right?"

Anisia stepped into her path and scowled. "The curse is not ridiculous. It's a fact. We've been living with its effects for centuries now, and we all know that until it's broken, the chances of any of us becoming pregnant are practically nil."

Tess raised an eyebrow and shot the other woman's flat stomach a pointed look. "Apparently not, if what you're telling me is true. But either way, it's none of my business; first because I don't know you, and second because I can guarantee you that I have not broken any curses lately. Now get out of my way so can I go put an icepack on my entire body. Thanks."

"It doesn't matter if you know me; you know the Felix, and that's the part that matters in all this."

"No, actually, it doesn't, because *I did not break the curse.*"

"Then explain to me how the hell I got knocked up."

"Okay, it's like this. When a mommy and a daddy love each other very much, sometimes they want to exp—"

"Great, you're a frickin' comedian," Anisia said, still refusing to move out of Tess's path. "Notice how hard I'm not laughing. I'm twenty-seven years old. I've been sexually active since I was eighteen. In that time, I've had relationships with four different Felines and never taken a single precaution. I mean, why would I bother? My mom started trying to get pregnant when she was twenty-four and didn't have me till she was almost forty. It just doesn't happen for us without a damned long concerted effort. Until you showed up."

"Look, I know you must be—"

"Shut up. I'm telling you, you're the only thing that's changed here. Before you, there was nothing in this world safer than sex with a spotted Feline. Now? One lousy week of *you* and suddenly I'm about to be a frickin' mommy! Do you have any idea what that means?"

"I'm not—"

"Shut up. I had plans, you know. I have a good job with an ad agency in Midtown. I've been busting my ass for them for nearly four years, and I'm finally— *finally*—on the fast track to the promotion I deserved two years ago. I have plans, damn it, and they don't involve taking six weeks of maternity leave while some young, white, male asshole from Yale swoops in on an internship and steals *my* accounts!"

"What do you think—"

"I said, *shut. Up.* Don't go telling me that I should just get rid of it. That's bullshit. This is a *baby*. It's *my baby,* not to mention one of the first spotted Felines conceived this year. This is the future of my goddamned race we're talking about, and I am damned well going to keep it and raise it and love it like a mother ought to do. But you need to understand that this was Not. In. My. *Plan!*"

Anisia punctuated each statement with an increase in volume until Tess found herself stepping backward simply to preserve her ability to hear.

"Lady, you have got to get a grip on yourself." Tess retreated an extra step for good measure and eyed the other woman warily. "I sympathize with what you're telling me, really I do, but I think you need to stop for a minute and take a good look at the situation."

"Oh, I've looked plenty—"

Tess snapped and gave a pretty respectable growl of her own. "No, now it's your turn to shut up. I'm sorry if you think you're stuck with an unplanned pregnancy and all the consequences that go along with it, you but need to stop blaming it on me and maybe think about the fact that anyone who has un-protected sex with a fertile member of the opposite sex should maybe think about the repercussions, no matter how unlikely they might be."

"I told—"

"Zip it! You also apparently have a lot to learn about your own culture, sweet cheeks, because the legend *I* heard says that a spotted Feline has to re-main faithful to his human mate for a year and a day before everyone can get on with the baby making. Since none of you Others appears to be able to work out the technical aspects of a *calendar,* allow me to point out that far from three-hundred-sixty-odd days so far, it has been exactly *nine*. Now, why don't you go share that with your little friends and pass on the message that I said you can all start leaving me the hell alone? *Capice?*"

Sucking in a deep breath, Tess released it with a strangled groan and set off for her apartment as fast as her injured leg would carry her.

For the first block and a half, she paid more attention to listening for anyone approaching behind her than she did to the route home, which she knew like the back of her hand. She honestly wasn't sure whether the irritated and irritating Ms. Cuma would actually take her at her word and go back to wherever she'd come from, and she really didn't think she could take any more surprises tonight.

Come to think of it, she didn't think she could take much more of anything tonight.

By the time she turned the corner onto her own block, Tess felt ready to curl up in a little ball and whimper like an abandoned kitten. Her thigh ached so badly she knew the bruise she would find there must go all the way to the bone, and her back and shoulder felt like someone had beaten them with a lead pipe. Appropriately enough. All she wanted was a hot bath, a cold compress, and an entire bottle of extra-strength Advil. Not necessarily in that order.

Hell, she'd take them in any order she could get them.

Her left hand fumbled in her pocket for her key

ring, a task made doubly awkward by the facts that she kept her keys in her right pocket and that her right shoulder screamed like a banshee every time she so much as jostled that arm. After three painful attempts, she finally managed to pinch the fob between two fingers and palm the keys. She was trying to fit the key to the outer door lock when a large, masculine hand covered hers and squeezed.

This time, Tess didn't scream. She whimpered.

"What is the matter, *gatita*?"

Rafe's voice held only mild concern as he stepped up behind her, taking away the keys and opening the door himself. He ushered her into the building and the bright lights of the lobby area. When he caught a glimpse of her face, he cursed like a stevedore.

"What in the name of God happened to you?" he demanded in a roar loud enough to wake every occupant of the building.

The building across the street, that is.

Tess flinched. She'd had enough of being yelled at for the evening, thank you very much. Ignoring her irate lover, she limped over to the elevator and pressed the button with her left hand.

"Tessa," Rafe snarled, reaching out with the intent of turning her to face him. He didn't abandon the plan when she cried out, but he did hiss something in Spanish that she decided it was just as well she couldn't translate.

"Tessa," he repeated, his voice hard and deep and

menacing. "Don't ignore me. Tell me what happened to you. *Now*."

Tess shot him a glare and stepped out of the elevator as soon as it stopped on her floor. He followed so close behind her that she thought they might have stepped into her apartment at the exact same time, laws of physics be damned.

"I got mugged," she said resentfully, her left hand fumbling with the buttons on her coat. "Some guy came up behind me as I was walking home from the subway and took a couple of swings at me. I got a flash that something was about to happen right before it did, so I managed to duck the worst of the initial blow, otherwise I'd have been knocked unconscious."

Or worse.

Rafe looked grimmer than any reaper could hope for. He brushed her hands away and eased her coat off himself, his sharp eyes noting the way she winced whenever she had to shift her right arm or shoulder. He didn't stop with the coat, though, just shifted his hands to the buttons on her shirt and began flicking those open as well. Fatigue began to settle on Tess, taking away her ability to protest. She simply stood there and let him undress her in the middle of her living room.

"What did he look like?"

Tess shook her head. "I didn't get a good look. He came up behind me, like I said, and he was wearing a jacket with a hood pulled all the way up. Plus, it looked like he had a bandanna wrapped around his face, like some kind of gangster. That's probably what he was, some gang member looking for money or street cred or something. He only got in two hits before someone saw and scared him off."

Rafe dropped her blouse on the floor and unsnapped her bra, easing it down her arms before tossing it aside. Gently he turned her to the side so he could assess the damage to her back and shoulder. He said nothing, but Tess could feel the rage billowing off him like clouds of steam. He hadn't been this angry when he caught her tailing him. Not even close.

He trailed his fingertips over her shoulder in a feather-light caress. It still made her hiss in discomfort.

"You said two hits." His voice sounded strangely flat, but it didn't take a genius to realize that he'd grasped the reins of his temper in an iron grip. "Where else did he strike you?"

Tess ventured a quick glance at his face and knew that now was not the time to assert her independence.

"On my leg," she admitted. "My left thigh."

He said nothing, simply sank down to kneel at her feet and reached for the fastening of her jeans. He had them open and sliding down her hips in the space of a few heartbeats, taking her panties with them. He grasped each ankle in turn and helped her step out of the pooled fabric. Them he lifted his eyes to her left thigh and surveyed the damage.

Unlike the blow to her back, this time Tess could

see the marks left by her attacker. A thick, black bruise ringed by an angry red halo had already begun to form against her pale skin. About two inches wide and eight inches long, the contusion angled down from her hip and across the front of her leg, pointing vaguely toward the opposite knee. It looked nasty and painful and Tess knew it would hurt even more over the next few hours.

Rafe's fingertips traced the discoloration as lightly as a breath, and Tess could see the muscles in the side of his jaw jumping as he struggled to maintain his composure. Somehow, knowing that he felt such anger on her behalf made her own anger at her unknown assailant lessen. He had taken the burden on himself.

Tess lifted her left hand to brush over his silky dark hair. "I know it looks terrible, and I can't say it doesn't hurt like a sonuvabitch, but it's not serious, Rafe. Nothing is broken, and the bruising will fade in a couple of weeks. I'll be fine."

He said nothing for a long moment, just stared at her injury and soothed it with barely there caresses. Tess watched his golden eyes glow intently with emotion and wanted suddenly to wrap her arms around him, to be the one to offer *him* comfort.

"I should have been there," he finally rumbled, his voice hoarse and thick with gravel. "I should have been there to protect you. No one should be allowed to harm you, *gatita*. I would kill any man who tried."

She opened her mouth to respond, a thoughtless platitude or a flippant remark ever on the tip of her tongue, but something stopped her. Maybe it was the fierce tenderness that turned his gaze into molten gold, or maybe it was the fist of something powerful and frightening that tightened around her own heart. Either way, Tess found herself at a loss for words.

She gazed down into those beautiful old-gold eyes and suffered another clench of that fist. It was getting harder and harder to pretend that what she felt every time she looked at him wasn't deep, irrevocable love.

Just the thought made her tremble, and Rafe interpreted the movement as cold or shock or pain, because he stood and swept her carefully into his arms, cradling her against him warmth like a precious treasure.

"You're safe now," he murmured. "No one will ever harm you again, *gatita*. I will not allow it. I will take care of you. I will keep you safe. I promise."

It would be so easy to let herself believe that those intensely spoken words of possession and protection meant Rafe loved her, Tess realized. If she allowed herself, she could move forward happily believing that this ultimate tomcat loved her enough to put aside all other women and be hers alone for the rest of their lives.

God, how she would love to believe that was true.

The way her heart jumped at the thought told Tess how far she had already fallen. She'd be lucky if she ever saw the surface again. But that didn't mean she couldn't maintain her dignity. She didn't have to act like an idiot just because she'd fallen head over heels in love with a man who redefined the notion that "men just aren't monogamous animals." She could at least try to maintain a semblance of dignity. And she could begin by putting her foot down when the feel of his arms around her began to make her knees go as weak as water.

"Rafe, I said I'd be fine, and I meant it," she said, pushing at his shoulders in an attempt to separate them by at least the width of a sheet of paper. "All I need is a hot bath and some of my arnica-and-comfrey liniment. That will help with both the pain and the bruising and will even get some of the swelling down. I keep a jar of it in the bathroom. Just let me go get it and get the bath running, and I'll be fine. You'll see."

He shook his head and thwarted her attempts to get him to release her. Instead, he adjusted his grip and scooped her up in his arms like a swooning damsel in distress.

"I will run your bath," he informed her, carrying her toward the bathroom, his face set in an expression of stalwart determination. "And I will apply your salve. I might not have been there to protect you earlier, *gatita,* but at least I can be here to care for you now."

"Rafe, really. That's not necessary. I'm perfectly capable of taking care of myself."

"I never said otherwise, though I would like to point out that the wound on your back would require the flexibility of a contortionist for you to be able to tend it on your own. I know you can take care of yourself, but tonight I would very much like if you would allow *me* to take care of you."

Tess saw the sincerity and tenderness in his eyes and felt her heart melt a little more. How was she supposed to resist this man?

Why would she want to?

"Well," she said, her strength waning, "I suppose you could help me with the salve, at least. I mean, if you really want to."

"I want to," he confirmed, setting her down on the fluffy rug beside the bath and squeezing her arms gently. "Believe me when I tell you, *gatita*, that caring for you will be entirely my pleasure."

Eighteen

Rafe's pleasure apparently also involved licking every square inch of her body with that rough sandpaper-velvet tongue.

Not that he mentioned that until later. Much later. First he let her soak in the tub for what seemed like forever, the gently steaming water loosening her abused muscles and soothing the sting of the deep, violent bruises. When she felt nearly as relaxed as warm molasses, he picked up a washcloth and a bar of her lemon balm soap and began to wash her with all the gentle patience of a mama cat caring for her kittens. Finally, after he'd rinsed her clean, he bundled her up in a nest of warm towels and carried her into the shadowy recesses of her bedroom.

He laid her on the cotton sheets as if laying her on an altar, all tenderness and reverence and warm, gentle hands. With infinite care, he opened the jar of arnica-and-comfrey salve she had given him earlier and began to smooth it onto her injuries. He kept his touch light, murmuring soothing nonsense when she winced at even his careful pressure on her abused shoulder and thigh. Still he spread the balm thoroughly to allow the herbs to work their magic. When he finished, he began to massage her unwounded muscles, making them go limp and heavy with pleasure. His warm, slick hands held magic of their own—powerful magic—as they kneaded every last bit of tension from her back, arms, and legs.

By the time he flipped her over and began to smooth his palms over her chest and stomach, she couldn't decide if she wanted to fall asleep or yank him down to her and indulge in some vigorous exercise. Judging by the expression he wore, he knew perfectly well what she was thinking, and he had his own answer to her conundrum.

His eyes glinted in the darkness while his hands skimmed her flesh, not so much touching her as waking her up to his touch. Where his hands went, they left her skin aching and sensitive.

"Keep still," he purred. "You need to be careful of your injuries. I never want you to feel pain while you are in my arms, *gatita*."

Tess shivered when he moved away, the loss of his radiant heat chilling her. Right now she could barely remember her injuries. All she could feel was him.

She stayed where he had placed her while he moved to either side of the bed, adjusting the lamps that sat there to dim golden glows. The light made his skin glow almost copper in places, and shadowed it in deep, aged bronze in others. All planes and angles, he was gorgeous in her eyes, the perfect figure of a man. She shivered again, this time in anticipation.

"If you don't hurry, I'll be really still." Her voiced sounded husky in her own ears. "As in asleep."

He chuckled and rounded the end of the bed, climbing onto it and prowling toward her on all fours, looking a lot like he had the other day, when he'd sported three-inch fangs and a thick, plush layer of fur. "Oh, I don't think so, sweet Tess. I think you'll be wide awake for as long as I want."

She wondered if her own eyes could flare as brightly as his, or if that was just a Feline thing. "Really? I guess that's up to you, then. If you give me a reason to stay awake . . ."

"I'll give you plenty."

That's when he set his tongue to the skin inside the arch of her foot and licked.

Tess moaned.

She'd heard of foot fetishes, of course, but she'd never really taken them seriously. After all, how sexy could a foot possibly be? For heaven's sake, she spent most of her time walking on them. Aside from providing a means of locomotion to get her to a chosen partner, what the heck could they possibly have to do with sex?

Under the stroke of Rafe's tongue, they had everything to do with it. They felt like satellite sex organs, each flick and rub and nibble sending pleasure shooting from her feet directly to her core. He bit delicately in the middle of the arch, and she got wet. He scraped his teeth across her sole, and she quivered. He licked the base of her toes and she could feel her clit throbbing in response. The man had more magic in the tip of his tongue than she had in her entire, aroused, aching, needy body.

"Reason number one, sweet Tess." His growl had the same rough-smooth texture as his tongue and drove her almost as crazy. "Shall we move on to number two?"

She whimpered in reply, then stuffed her fist into her mouth to stifle any more embarrassing and revealing sounds. Luckily even in her aroused state, she'd known better than to move her right arm. She had to settle for the left.

"Ah-ah," he chided, dragging her hand slowly back to the mattress. "I said stay still. And I want to hear those noises. They're part of the fun."

"I'll give you more than noise in just a minute if you don't—"

Her useless threat strangled in her throat when he closed his teeth around the back of her ankle and began nibbling his way north. "Ah!"

He chuckled and massaged her calf with long, thorough strokes of his tongue.

Tess lay back on the bed and tried to think of England, or muggings, or quantum physics, but all she could really think about was the shift and slide of his mouth up toward her knees. His teeth and lips and tongue all conspired to cause her downfall.

What else could she think when he found a particularly sensitive spot at the back of her right knee and proceeded to exploit it with nibbles and scrapes and sweet hot suction until she actually cried out. From having her knees nibbled!

"Rafe! Stop it! Just stop!" Her breath was coming fast now, and she sounded panting and eager. Probably because she was both. "Stop teasing me and get up here."

He shook his head, his thick, dark hair caressing her thighs as he laved his way around her knee to her inner thigh, taking care to avoid her livid bruise. "Can't. Busy."

"Argh! Busy my ass!"

He lifted his head, grinned at her, and shook his head again. "Not yet. I've got other things to do first."

Then he lowered his head, and she felt his tongue glide in one, long drag from her knee across her thigh to her waiting core.

He might as well have killed her.

She cried out like a murder victim, a long, high wail that begged for mercy. He showed her none. His tongue slid between her swollen folds, seeking out her very center and drinking from her like she was a fountain of cream. She could feel the vibrations of his rough purr traveling from her sex to her thundering heart. She groaned in response and whimpered when he dipped inside, tongue penetrating and thrusting into her in a breathtakingly intimate kiss.

Orders be damned. She buried her hands in his

hair, desperate to have something to hold on to while her world spun dangerously out of control. She could barely feel the tight strain of her bruised shoulder muscles. She couldn't even feel the mattress beneath her. All she could feel was Rafe's mouth and teeth and tongue and hands and breath and purr wreaking havoc inside her.

"Please! Rafe, please. I need—" She arched into a bow as his tongue curled around her most sensitive nub and tugged with agile precision. "God, I need you! Please—"

"I am pleasing you," he murmured, shifting a hand between her thighs. "And you're going to come for me. Now."

He thrust two fingers high and deep inside her and she had no choice but to obey. "More," he growled.

She rained down on him like April, flooding his hand with cream and his ears with a torrent of gasping cries. She screamed his name. She screamed to God. She screamed for mercy. But mostly she screamed for more. He gave it to her.

More.

Eyes feasting on her, Rafe gave her another finger and watched a new wave of convulsions seize her. He could feel her inner muscles clench around his fingers like a fist, then the tensing and release of her climax. Her moisture slicked his palm. He bent his head to lap it up, thick as cream, sweet as honey, and rich as her scent. He couldn't get enough.

More.

He ignored the cries for mercy, the way her ragged breath soughed in and out of her lungs. He could hear her exhaustion, and he didn't care. He wanted more, wanted to claim her, to erase the nightmare of her attack, the pain of her poor, battered muscles. Leaning down, he drew her tiny bud into his mouth and suckled it like a nipple. Her muscles clenched around his fingers again, a new wave driving her back into climax before she'd barely begun to descend.

More.

Her fingers knotted in his hair and jerked painfully. Rafe ignored them. He ignored the burning in his scalp and the ringing cries in his ears. He ignored the bite of her nails into his shoulder when one hand clutched at him, frantic and grasping. He just bit down on her sensitive flesh and drove her over another peak.

More.

She began to cry, gasping sobs shaking her as tears tracked down her cheeks to the sheets beneath her head. He saw it and he knew he should ease off on her, but he couldn't. His instincts rode him hard, ignoring the reason of the man in favor of the hunger of the beast. The beast wanted him to mark her, mark her and keep her forever, permanently hot and wet and aching for him. He flexed his fingers and touched her deeper.

More.

Her hands curled into fists and beat at his shoulders, and still he pressed her. Up and up and up until she stopped coming down. Her climax had become one huge, unending orgasm from which she couldn't break free, because he was constantly there to drag her back. Her voice went hoarse from begging, but it seemed to make no difference. He had no mercy. He growled at her pleas and pushed her higher.

More.

Then, abruptly, she stopped struggling. The fight went out of her and she lay still on the sweaty, tangled sheets. Her thighs fell open, leaving her totally exposed. Her hands dropped to her sides and her eyelids fluttered closed. Her dry lips parted, and it was her whisper that brought him back to reason.

"I love you, Rafe."

He froze, fingers buried between her smooth, bruised thighs, tongue dancing across her creamy center. Her words flashed a lightning bolt of pride and fierce satisfaction inside him, and they brought him a new and unexpected peace.

Gently, he eased his hand away from her, sliding up the mattress until their bodies were aligned and he could take her into his arms, cradling her close. Grasping her uninjured thigh in his hand, he lifted it over his and pulled her hips against his until he could slip inside gently and easily. Her hands came up to push him away, but he refused her. He shushed her with soothing whispers and soft promises and rocked slowly against her, not thrusting, but reveling in the connection between their two bodies. When the climax came this time, it was the gentle ripple of a pond, no more violent than a heartbeat and just as comforting.

He hugged her to him and tried not to panic.

Then he tried not to love her and panic became inevitable.

"Rafe," she breathed.

"Shhh." He brushed her hair away from her forehead, smoothing the tousled curls and pressing a soft kiss to the damp skin beneath. "I'm right here, my sweet Tess. Right exactly here."

She slipped breathlessly into sleep, and he followed soon after, still joined, body-to-body, skin-to-skin, heart-to-heart.

Nineteen

Rafe woke with a purr, a deep, reverberating sound of contentment that started somewhere down around his toes and ended several inches above what he could only assume to be a cat-and-canary smile. Today everything felt right with his world. Including the warm, soft bundle that currently rested against his chest. That felt the rightest of all.

His eyes drifted open and went immediately to Tess. With her face buried in the pillow and her body half turned away from him, all he could really see was her tousled curls and the pale skin of her neck rising free of the rumpled sheets. The sight still made him purr even louder. She looked right lying beside him, as if she belonged there. As if she should never sleep anywhere else.

And wasn't that a kick in the pants, as others might say? Who would have thought that Rafael De Santos, tomcat, Romeo, and all-around bachelor would ever fall in love, especially with a witch of a woman who seemed to enjoy arguing with him as much as she enjoyed making love with him? He certainly had never seen her coming.

But then, what man ever saw his future until it appeared before him as the present moment? Premonition wasn't a gift common to his kind—wasn't a common gift at all, really—and even if he had known that Fate was sneaking up on him, he couldn't honestly say he would have done anything different.

Although, speaking of premonitions . . .

His purr rumbled to a stop in his chest as he drew the sheet farther down Tess's back and saw the evidence of the attack she'd survived the night before. The back of her right shoulder bore a nasty bruise the color of rotting meat—black and purple with traces of red and yellowish green around the edges. Just the sight of it made him want to rip someone's throat out, preferably whoever had dared to lay a hand on her, but honestly at the moment he didn't feel all that picky.

Tess had said she never saw the face of her attacker, but she had also said that she'd seen the first blow coming before it hit. Now, looking at the damage the pipe had done to her shoulder and back, Rafe offered up a silent prayer of thanks that the blow hadn't landed on her skull. If it had, she would have died almost immediately. And then something inside Rafe would have died as well.

"I can feel you staring," she grumbled, not bothering to lift her face out of the pillow. It muffled her voice, but his Feline hearing had no trouble picking out her words. "I'd say it's not as bad as it looks, but since I can't see it and it still aches like a sore tooth, I can't seem to muster up the energy to lie."

Rafe felt his mouth quirk. It amazed him the way she could make him want to smile even while he continued to contemplate ways to find her attacker and rend him limb from limb.

He leaned down and feathered a kiss over the tender skin. "You never need to lie to me, sweet Tess. If you are in pain, I wish to know. Should I apply more of your salve?"

She turned her head and pushed a tumble of curls out of her eyes so she could blink up at him from beneath sleep-heavy eyelids. "It can't hurt, and it might help with the aching. You remember which jar?"

Rafe lifted it from the bedside table where he'd placed it the night before. "I have it here. Shoulder first."

A small hiss escaped her when he first spread the thick unguent over her bruised muscle, but he murmured something soothing and kept his touch as careful as he could. He hated the idea of causing her more pain in the healing process almost as much as he hated the idea that she'd been injured in the first place. He had meant his words of the previous night: He should have been there to protect her.

She was his to protect.

He felt her begin to relax under his hands and smoothed on the last bit of salve, rubbing gently to ensure it penetrated into the muscle. It impressed him that the medicinal balm absorbed into the skin more like a lotion than a greasy ointment, and he found the crisp, herbal fragrance both refreshing and unobtrusive. No wonder his *gatita*'s store appeared so successful, if she had the talent to produce products like this one. Pride warmed his chest and he had to remind himself to focus on the task at hand.

"Turn over now. Your leg next."

Tess obeyed with a lazy grumble and shifted onto her back even as she kept the sheet pinned to her chest. The gesture made Rafe smile.

"So shy, *gatita*?" he teased. "Do you not remember all the places I saw last night? All the places I touched? And tasted?"

He leaned close and nuzzled the sensitive hollow beneath her ear, which earned him a hunched shoulder and a slap on the chest.

"Hey, back off, Garfield," she scowled, but he saw the flash of warmth in her eyes and knew she wanted him as constantly as he wanted her. "Between the mugging I got on the street last night and the workout you put me through when I got home, I think I'm entitled to a day of rest here, all right?"

A chuckle of delight escaped him. He took no offense at her words. He could see in the delicate color beneath her eyes and the pale tone of her skin that his Tess really was tired, but he could smell in her fragrance that she still wanted him. That knowledge satisfied him for the moment.

Still, if he needed to strip away her covering in

order to tend to her wounds . . . well, anything in the name of good health, yes?

She clung to the cotton with the tenacity of a dog with a bone. "Hey, I said give it a rest!"

Rafe clucked at her and shook his head, but he couldn't quite suppress his smile. "You wound me, *gatita*. I am simply attempting to care for your injuries. I would assume that this healing cream is less effective when applied through a layer of cloth. Am I right?"

She glared.

"Now, now, be a good girl," he urged, tugging at the thin fabric covering. "If you behave and take your medicine, maybe you will get a special surprise later on. How does that sound?"

Tess snorted and dropped her gaze between his legs. "Less than surprising," she grumbled drily.

He chuckled. He couldn't help it. When he was with Tess, he always felt like laughing. She did that to him.

"Get your mind out of the gutter, sweet Tess. I had something more like ice cream in mind. But I suppose that if you insist . . ."

"Oh, just give me that," she snapped, holding a hand out for the salve. "I can take care of my thigh without your help."

He turned serious. "But it gives me pleasure to help you. If I could not be there to prevent your injuries, then I at least need to be the one to tend to them. Please."

The *please* seemed to act like a key in a lock, doing away with Tess's irritable expression and making her soften back into the bed.

"Fine. Do your worst," she said.

"Only my best for you, *gatita*."

She let him draw the sheet down to the foot of the bed, her only protest the rosy flush of color that stained her cheeks and her chest with heat. Rafe found the sight entrancing. He couldn't stop himself from taking a moment to drink in her beauty, all soft and warm and spread out before him like a saucer of heated cream. With her fair skin, golden hair, and blue eyes, she looked so different from him, so much smaller and more delicate. Fragile, even. When he put his hands on her, he marveled at the contrasts between them, then marveled again at how right it felt to touch her. Like she belonged.

To him.

Tess cleared her throat nervously, and Rafe offered her a reassuring smile. Dragging his attention back to her wounds, he surveyed the damage to her luscious, curved thigh. The bruise there had come up sooner, so he'd seen more of it yesterday than he had on the one on her shoulder. He had to admit that while it still looked painful—and apparently felt that way, judging by the way she drew in a sharp breath when he touched it—the salve did appear to have sped the healing up a little. Rafe could see larger margins of yellow, green, and gray around the perimeter of the bruise, signs of later stages of healing. Grunting in satisfaction, he began smoothing the salve onto her skin.

"I am still not convinced you should not see a doctor," he said, scooping up another dollop of goo.

Tess propped herself up on her elbows to watch his treatment. "I told you, I'm fine. Nothing is broken, and a doctor can do less for deep bruising than I can do for myself. I just need a few days for the swelling to go down, and they won't even hurt anymore. Trust me."

Rafe did trust her; he trusted her with his very heart, but that didn't mean he didn't feel the urge to wrap her up in cotton wool to ensure no harm ever touched her. He never wanted to let her out of his sight.

He opened his mouth to speak, to try to tell her what she had come to mean to him, but the strident peal of the doorbell cut him off.

Tess frowned and glanced at the clock. "It's barely nine o'clock on a Saturday morning. Who the heck is at my front door?"

She swung her legs to the side of the bed and stood, hurrying over to her closet to grab a long, cotton robe off its hanger. Rafe already had his trousers on and busied himself fastening the buttons.

"I'll see who it is," he said and left the bedroom before she could stop him.

He heard her protests but ignored them. Instinct, deep and primitive, made him determined to place himself between Tess and any intruder. He didn't care if it was her best friend at the door; from now on, anyone who wanted to see Tess would have to go through him.

Unfortunately, the door opened not on Tess's best friend, but on her grandfather.

"Mr. Menzies," he said smoothly, or as smoothly as he could while standing half naked in the living room of the visitor's only grandchild. "What a surprise. Would you like to come in?"

Lionel pushed through the door with little grace.

"I can't say I'm surprised, unfortunately," the old man snapped, planting himself in the living room so firmly, Rafe would not have been surprised to see roots growing into the carpet. "I was afraid this had happened. And to think I rushed all the way to this ghetto in the hope I could stop it before it was too late."

"Granddad?"

Both men turned at the sound of Tess's voice. She stood framed in the door to her bedroom with one hand clutching the sides of her robe closed in front of her. The pale blue material covered her from neck to toenails, but she didn't appear comfortable with her appearance. Maybe because she and Rafe both looked as if they had just rolled out of bed.

Her bed.

"Tessa," Lionel acknowledged coldly. "I would ask for the meaning of this, but it would only serve to insult us both. The evidence does, as they say, speak for itself."

Rafe saw Tess flinch and lift a hand to smooth back her hair. Her grandfather's words clearly affected her.

"Granddad, what are you doing here?" she asked, in a tone Rafe had never heard her use before. She sounded subdued, almost deferential. As far as he knew, his Tess never deferred to anyone.

"I hardly think why I came is the central issue, now that I've been greeted by this little scene." Lionel gave Rafe an insulting visual once-over, then focused on his granddaughter with a haughty glare of disdain. "Really, Tessa. I've never credited you with much discrimination when it came to your personal life, but this? This is outrageous. You've given yourself to an animal. You couldn't find yourself a man of at least the same species? Even an unmagical human would have been better than this."

Tess must have heard Rafe growl, because she shot him a quelling look and gestured for him to stay where he was. "I didn't think you had any interest in my personal life, Granddad. You rarely ask me about it anymore, after all."

"Why should I bother to ask? I know the answers would only disappoint me," the old man glowered. "I did my best to steer you you in the proper direction while you were under my roof. I raised you, I dressed you, I introduced you to all the right people. And how did you repay me? You did nothing to secure the proper sort of husband I tried to steer you toward. You could have been the wife of a councilor, and instead you chose to defy me and become some sort of hippie, selling herbs and potions like some medieval peasant woman. That was humiliation enough. But this?" He waved a hand toward Rafe. "This is too much."

While he had decided long ago that people who threw around such nasty words were not worth listening to, Rafe now learned that hearing them spoken to his woman made him want to rip out the tongue that uttered them. Only Tess stepping forward to place a hand on his arm held him back.

"This? You might think it's 'too much,' but you don't seem surprised by it," she said, her voice quiet but calm. Only through her touch on his bare arm could he feel the tension that gripped her. "In fact, you seem as if you already knew Rafe and I had formed a relationship over the past couple of weeks. How is that, Granddad? We haven't exactly been painting the town red these days."

"You can't hide these things from me, Tessa. I always find out." Lionel's blue eyes speared into her, and Rafe had to fight back the urge to step between the two family members, to protect Tess from the man who had raised her. "As it happens, I began to suspect something when I encountered your animal friend here at the Vircolac Club. Your energy clung to his aura like dryer lint. I had intended to prepare him for his meeting with the council, but now I'm no longer sure that meeting should even take place. Not only has De Santos compromised his impartiality by consorting with a member of our community, such as she is, but from what I saw at the club, he can't even control his own animalistic tendencies. As far as I'm concerned, I should go straight back to the Witches' Council and advise them to rethink their request to meet with the Others. Especially with an Other like this."

Once again, Tess held him back. His jaguar chafed at the restraint, at being asked to allow his mate to be insulted in his presence. The beast wanted to teach Lionel Menzies some manners, preferably through the judicious use of claws and fangs. The man, however, realized that violence would solve nothing. It would only distress Tess and prove Lionel's point.

But that didn't mean Rafe had to be happy about the situation.

Beside him, Tess drew a slow, deep breath.

"Grandfather," she began, and he could hear how she had to strain to keep her tone level, "I doubt anyone cares whom I date enough to approve or disapprove. The only person who gets a say in how I run my life is me. Of course, I do try to take your feelings into consideration when I can, but—"

"You call *this* taking my feelings into consideration?"

"Maybe not, but I had no reason to believe you would have any feelings one way or the other. You're not usually very interested in my life. I, however, am interested in hearing about when you two ran into each other and why I'm only hearing about it now."

She cast Rafe a pointed look.

He raised her hand and brushed his lips over the backs of her fingers. "I am sorry, *gatita*. This happened yesterday afternoon, and it flew completely out of my head the moment I saw you again."

"Very touching," Lionel sneered. "And very smooth for a man I last encountered looking like an extra from a low-budget horror movie. Tell me, Tessa, do you find him equally attractive when his face is covered with yellow fur and black spots?"

Tess looked from Rafe to her grandfather and back again. "What is he talking about?"

"Nothing important. I was simply . . . not feeling well when your grandfather saw me—"

"What I saw was an animal walking on two legs. That might be something that you find attractive, Tessa, but I can assure you it will not appeal to the members of the Witches' Council. If we're going to throw our lot in with the Others, we would at least like to remain reasonably certain that they won't lose control and turn on us at any moment."

That was it.

Rafe bared his teeth at the older man. "Believe me when I tell you, Mr. Menzies, that if I were likely to turn on you, I would already have done so."

Tess shushed him. "Granddad, I don't know what you saw yesterday, because I wasn't there, but I do know Rafe, and I can assure you that he's not a threat to you or to any other member of the council. For pete's sake, do you think the Others would let him lead their Council if he really couldn't be relied on to control himself?"

"How should I know how those animals think?" Lionel demanded, stepping forward, his blue eyes shooting lasers at Rafe. "I can only base my opinions on what I can see, and what that tells me is that this man can't be trusted."

One more step and Lionel would be close enough to touch Tess, and that was something Rafe couldn't allow, not when anger held such a clear grip on the man. When the old witch moved again, Rafe stepped forward to place himself between him and Tess, inadvertently jerking on the hand that still gripped his bare arm. He heard her gasp and looked down to see all the color draining from her face.

He froze, instantly forgetting about Menzies and focusing all of his attention on his mate. "I am so sorry, *gatita*. I never meant to aggravate your injury. How badly does it hurt? Do you need to see a doctor this time?"

"What are you talking about? What injury?" Lionel demanded, shifting until he could see his granddaughter's face over the Feline's shoulder. "Tessa, did this animal hurt you?"

Rafe gave a muffled roar at the very idea, but Tess was already shaking her head.

"No, Granddad, Rafe didn't hurt me," she said. "I was mugged last night coming home. The guy who attacked me hit me a couple of times before someone scared him off. I'm just sore, is all. Sore and bruised.

I'm fine. And I don't need a doctor," she added, for Rafe's benefit.

"You don't need to lie to protect him, Tessa. If he injured you in any way—"

"Granddad!" Tess snapped, waiting until the man fell silent and frowned down at her. "I'm not lying. Rafe would never hurt me. In fact, he took care of me last night when I got home. That's why he stayed here last night—so he could look after me."

Rafe bit back to urge to clarify that it hadn't been the only reason he had stayed. Somehow, he didn't think Tess would appreciate the interjection.

"At this point, I don't think it's all that important what you believe," she said with a frown of her own. "What's important is that you have the courtesy to treat me and my guests with respect while you're in my home. Now might also be a good time for you to answer my original question: Why are you here, Granddad? You've always told me you'd rather be shot than step foot in my neighborhood. In fact, you seemed to think that if you did, you would be. So to what do I owe this surprise?"

Lionel glared at his granddaughter and tugged fiercely on his cuffs, aligning them precisely with the sleeves of his suit coat. "I had been asked to enlist you in delivering another message, but now that I see how close you are to the recipient, I can deliver it myself."

He turned to Rafe. "My colleagues were less than pleased when I told them of your loss of control yes-

terday, Mr. De Santos. It has raised some concern
among several of the council members. They feel it
might be prudent to meet you sooner than our next
scheduled meeting. I believe they may want to form
their own impressions of your suitability to handle
the intricacies of relations between our two councils.
I'm afraid they no longer feel your reputation pro-
vides them with sufficient reassurance as to your . . .
character."

The man knew how to deliver an insult without
uttering a single offensive word. Rafe had to give him
credit. He also had to remember not to punch him in
his supercilious face.

Rafe nodded abruptly. "Simply name the time, Mr.
Menzies, and I would be happy to personally assure
your colleagues that I am more than capable of han-
dling any challenges that might be thrown my way.
I am at your disposal, as it were."

"Tomorrow night." The other man threw the words
out as if they left a bad taste in his mouth. "After they
meet you, the council will decide whether or not to
call on you to attend the full moon sitting."

Lionel turned to Tess with a look of disgust. "As
for you, Tessa, I believe the council has a word or
two for you, as well. I'm sure you won't mind escort-
ing your animal lover to the council chambers. Not
after he's . . . taken such good care of you."

Rafe could scent the hurt and anger that Lionel's
behavior caused for Tess, but she said not a word.
She simply nodded to acknowledge the summons

and crossed to the apartment door, yanking it open and fixing her relative with a meaningful stare.

"Good-bye, Granddad," she said, lifting her chin and squaring her shoulders despite the discomfort Rafe knew the movement must have caused. "You can tell the council that your message was received."

Rafe knew more than one had been.

Lionel didn't bother to say good-bye, just strode out of the apartment as if the air were unfit to breathe. He never bothered to look at Tess's face and never saw the hurt he had caused to the child he'd raised.

Rafe waited for her to close the door, then drew her into his arms and rocked her against his chest. "I am sorry, my sweet *gatita*. He does not deserve a grandchild like you. You are too fine for such an angry and bitter old man."

Her arms came around him and clung, and she sniffled against his chest. "I've always known I was a disappointment to him. He's made that abundantly clear over the years, but I never realized he might actually hate me. What could I have done to make him hate me? Because clearly it started before you came along."

Rafe stroked a hand over her springy curls and murmured soothing words. He ached that he was unable to take away her pain.

"It is not you, *gatita*. Some men are simply incapable of loving anyone but themselves. To some, appearances mean more than the truth of a person's heart. If your grandfather could see your heart, he would know how amazing you truly are."

"Thank you for saying that." She tilted her head back and offered him a watery smile. "And especially thank you for making it sound so sincere."

"It was sincere. *I* am sincere."

In fact, he sincerely wanted to wipe away the tracks of her tears with his tongue. Then he wanted to go rip the heart right out of Lionel Menzies's chest, but he couldn't do that. Sometimes being the head of the Council of Others felt entirely too restrictive.

She stared up at him for a moment, her blue eyes shining brightly from her tears. She seemed to search his soul with them, and all Rafe could do was hope she understood how much she had come to mean to him. How sincerely he needed her.

"You know," she said slowly, reaching up to stroke his face with cool, slender fingers. "I honestly think you mean that."

"Of course I do, *gatita*. You amaze me every day. Every moment. Over and over again."

He leaned down and brushed her lips with a kiss full of reverence and awe. This woman had burrowed her way into his heart, and once he had performed this latest duty to the Council, he would make certain she knew it.

"In fact," he told her, drawing back and wiping a stray tear away with his thumb, "I cannot wait to stand before this Witches' Council with you at my side, sweet Tess. Even if your grandfather is too ignorant to recognize your value, I refuse to believe that thirteen men of sufficient intelligence to govern their kind will be as well. They, too, will have to be in awe of your power."

She laughed then, a spontaneous belly laugh that opened her mouth wide and left her ginning up at him. "Oh, Rafe. I hate to disappoint you, baby, but I've known most of the councilmen since I was in diapers, and awe is not the emotion they usually feel when they see me. And power never plays into it. As far as they're concerned the power I have isn't enough to light a candle. I'm afraid if you're expecting them to disagree with my grandfather's assessment of me, you're doomed to disappointment."

"Never." He leaned down and kissed her smiling mouth, unable to resist. She lit his heart up when she smiled. "Your grandfather's friends might confuse magic with power, but I am not so foolish. When I say you have power, *gatita,* I mean every word of it. You fairly shimmer with the stuff."

She slapped his shoulder lightly. "Don't tease. I've told you I'm sensitive about my abilities as a witch. Or rather, my lack of abilities. You shouldn't make fun."

"I am not. I am completely in earnest. You, my sweet Tess, have to learn to stop underestimating yourself, and if you refuse to do it on your own, I have a feeling that one of these days Fate will step in and teach you this lesson the hard way."

She snickered. "Oh, so now you think you're the

one who has premonitions? Way to co-opt the only real magic I have, mister. That's real smooth."

Rafe swept her up into his arms and began carrying her back toward the bedroom. It was Saturday, after all, and he could think of no better way to relax after a busy week than in his mate's comfortable bed.

"It is not a premonition," he told her as he laid her down on the mattress and reached for the tie of her robe. "It is merely a statement of fact. You *will* recognize your power one of these days, *gatita,* and I only hope that I will be right there to see it."

Her gaze flickered to the side, then returned full of heat and mischief.

"Well, if you're so convinced I have magical powers," she purred, slipping her hand down between their bodies to curl around his growing erection, "then I'll just have to experiment to see if I can build them up, won't I? Now, I wonder what happens when I do . . . *this.*"

Her fingers flexed, and Rafe felt his eyes roll back in his head.

"Oh, I'll show you what happens," he growled, panting at the sudden surge of heat. "And after I have finished, you will never again doubt your own power."

"In that case"—she squeezed her fingers and reached up to nip at his mouth with playful intent— "what are you waiting for? Let my education begin."

Twenty

Tess had just slipped on her most conservative pearl earrings when she heard Rafe let himself into the apartment. She still wouldn't say she was entirely comfortable with the idea that they'd wound up all but living together barely two weeks into their relationship, but Rafe had ignored her every time she'd even thought about arguing. They had exchanged keys to their respective homes after three days of knowing each other, so she supposed she should just relax and go with the flow, especially considering she'd nearly given up on the idea of denying that she loved him. Fighting the emotion didn't seem to be doing her any good. When she had tried to keep him out of her apartment the first night after they'd met, he'd simply broken in, but Tess had been smart. She'd attached a small bell to his key chain along with her apartment key so that no matter whose place they were staying at, she'd always be able to hear him coming.

Hearing the sound of the cheerful little bell, she shoved her feet into her kidskin pumps and stepped out from behind the sofa to face the foyer. And the table she still couldn't look at without blushing.

"Hello, dear. How was your day?"

She felt very June Cleaver, meeting him at the door in pearls and a snappy dress, with her hair styled and heels on her feet, so she couldn't resist the classic greeting. She was betting, though, that June never laid one on Ward like she was kissing Rafe. The censors would have had a field day. Case in point: the way he kneaded her ass before setting her away from him and reaching down to adjust the fit of his tailored charcoal trousers.

"Not as good as I'm hoping my night will be." He frowned and reached out to tug at a severely styled curl. "What happened to your hair?"

Tess reached up to feel it self-consciously. The normally wild profusion of corkscrew curls had been brushed, rolled, set, and sprayed within an inch of their lives in preparation for her appearance in front of the firing squad—aka the Witches' Council.

"Nothing. I just tried to make it behave," she said. "Granddad hates when it looks all undisciplined."

"But I like it undisciplined. I especially like when it misbehaves. Like when I have you under me, and you're tossing your head against the pillows—"

Tess cleared her throat. Loudly. "Um, shouldn't we be going?"

He sighed. "I suppose if you insist, although I would be happy to develop an alternative plan for the evening."

"Down, boy. The council will not be happy if we show up late, or with our nice clothes all wrinkled."

He eyed her neat clothes, taking in the way the midnight-blue dress clung to her curves, all high-necked and short-sleeved like something Audrey Hepburn would wear. And she thought of that as one of her "unsexy" dresses. With the way he looked at her, she was beginning to think wearing her sexy dresses around him would be like pouring gasoline on a forest fire.

"All right," he agreed. "I'll be good. But only if you promise I can muss you later."

Tess ignored the way his smile always made her stomach clench, and the way he never talked about any emotions that weren't sexual. Like she'd told Missy, she would figure it all out later. After the council meeting.

"Show me you can earn it, and I just might."

He laughed and guided her to the elevator, then down to his waiting car. He'd left it running, with the key in the engine, and Tess just shook her head. It would never get stolen, that was for sure. But how the criminals knew Rafe was the driver while he was up inside the apartment, she could never get quite clear.

He was unusual just for having a car in Manhattan. Tess had long ago decided they weren't worth the trouble, but Rafe had offered an easy explanation. "There's no room in the city. When I need to run, I head upstate."

It explained the four-wheel drive, too.

Rafe drove like he did everything, lazily, gracefully, and with such a complete lack of haste you
never realized what was happening until it was all
over. All she did was give him the directions and he
had them weaving through traffic and navigating the
Upper West Side before she really had time to get
worked up about the coming meeting. But in the fifteen seconds between reverse and park, she more
than made up for that.

He pulled into a completely miraculous parking
spot, cut the engine, and turned to face her. "You are
beginning to panic. Stop it."

"I'm not panicking. I'm thinking."

"You are thinking panicked thoughts, then."

"My thoughts are none of your damned business."

"Of course they are. Especially when I have already told you not to panic."

"I don't take orders well at the best of times. In
case you hadn't noticed." She looked at him. "And
this isn't the best of times."

"Why not?"

She looked harder. "Let me think. Maybe because
I'm about to see my granddad for the second time in
a week, which is never good; I'm going to discuss an
issue of grave social, psychological, and martial im-
port, and said issue is likely to prove divisive and
heated. Oh, and I'm bring my lover, who happens to
be the very spokesman for the opposite side of said
issue, who has already made it clear that he loathes

him. Especially since he's a member of a different species." She pasted on a sickly false grin. "Sheesh! What have I got to worry about?"

Rafe chuckled and leaned forward to brush a kiss across her smiling mouth. "Relax. I told you, everything will be fine."

He slid out of his seat and walked around to her side to open her door. While she waited for him with her hands clenched into fists inside the long sleeves of her jacket, Tess snorted.

"Right. Now if only you'd told the same thing to my grandfather."

Tess had been to the council's meeting rooms a couple of times before, but never during an actual meeting. They were located in the basement of a series of row houses on a quiet street in not the best block of the Upper West Side. Not that the neighborhood was bad, but it bore an air of shabby gentility implying that it had seen its share of wealth—but a while ago. The slightly downtrodden air meant that no one took it amiss when an anonymous presence bought their homes and rented them back again with the basements tightly and irrevocably sealed off. With the exception of one, of course, and that's where Tess led Rafe.

She preceded him through the unmarked alley entrance around the side of the fifth house on the block. At the bottom of a dark, steep, narrow stairway, they stepped out into a small open area with floors and walls of bare concrete. A single, bare lightbulb swung from a wire in the ceiling. Tess felt Rafe's eyes on her as she walked to the only door in the room and raised her right hand to touch it precisely in its center. It swung open, and she waved him through, ignoring his raised eyebrow and curious stare.

"I thought you said you didn't do much magic?"

"I don't. I just let the magic that's already here read mine." Ignoring any further comments, as well as the huge knot in her stomach, Tess closed the door again behind them. By physically pushing it shut. "This way."

She felt a sense of urgency she couldn't define. Something told her she needed to hurry, but she'd glanced at her watch just a moment ago, and she knew she wasn't late. So what was going on?

Taking the lead once more, she hurried along the dingy corridor with its cement block walls until she came to a choice of passages. Straight ahead, she knew, lay an old wine cellar that now served as a storage room. The left passage led to a maze of corridors that never seemed to end, even if Tess knew it was an illusion meant to confuse anyone who happened to get past the door and wander down here uninvited. The council chamber was just a few dozen feet down the right-hand path. So why didn't Tess want to take it?

Rafe noticed her hesitation and frowned. "Is everything okay?"

Tess nodded her head. "Fine. I was just thinking for a second."

He raised an eyebrow. "You can't remember which way to go?"

"No, I remember. I'm just remembering something else, too."

"Like what?"

"Like, *duck!*"

Faster than she would have thought possible, Tess moved, throwing herself against Rafe so suddenly that she actually managed to knock him off balance. And that was good, because if he'd been on balance, there would have been a great big smoking hole right where his head had been. Tess knew that for a fact, because she could see it in the cement wall just beyond where his head and been.

"What the hell!"

That was just what Tess wanted to know, too, but at the moment she was too busy tugging Rafe down the center passage to bother asking. "Would you come on?" she hissed. "Something really weird is happening here."

Rafe growled and pushed her in front of him as they raced down the hall. "I figured that out when someone shot at us. That was someone shooting at us, was it not?"

"Well, he didn't have a gun, but otherwise, yeah, I'd say that was pretty accurate."

"Who is 'he,' precisely?"

Tess shoved the door of the wine cellar open and darted inside, urging Rafe in after her. As soon as he made it in, she slammed the door shut and began backing away from it.

"Tess," Rafe repeated impatiently. "Who is the 'he' who was shooting at us?"

She blinked. "My grandfather."

Twenty-one

Rafe just stared. He could not have just heard what he'd thought he'd heard. "Did you just say your grandfather is trying to kill us?"

He watched her jerky nod. She'd gone ghostly pale, and he thought he could see her skin glistening. He knew he could smell her fear.

"Yeah. I mean, technically, with that blow he was just trying to kill you, but the me part of us was definitely next on his agenda. Providing I'm remembering what I'm remembering fairly accurately."

"Do you usually? Remember accurately, I mean?"

"God, I hope not!"

"Why not?"

"Because I think I remember him killing me."

Rafe swore and shook his head. He refused to even contemplate the idea of Tess dying. It was not going to happen. Not for another sixty or seventy years at least. "What are you talking about? What are you remembering, Tess?"

She shuddered. "I told you when I see things, it's like seeing déjà vu a few seconds ahead of time. It's not enough time to change anything, just to get really scared. And to warn you that he won't hesitate. He won't think twice, so you can't count on him to."

"Tess! What the hell does that—?"

He never got to finish his question.

The door slammed open as if it had been kicked, catching Tess in the hip and sending her sprawling right into the path of the bolt of sickly green energy that shot from her grandfather's fingers in time to his half-chanted words. She took the blow directly to her chest, and Rafe saw the singe marks on her clothes when she went down. She hit the floor like a crash test dummy, and he roared in denial.

"She's not dead yet," Lionel Menzies drawled as he stepped into the small room. He had the sour smell of the mentally unbalanced and the rich, earthy fragrance of someone who was very clever indeed. "I'll get to that later, after I've dealt with matters between the two of us. Right now, you and I need to do a little negotiating."

Rafe tried to step toward Tess's limp form, but Lionel said a few words and suddenly there was a shimmering, malevolent green wall between Rafe and Tess.

"Ah, forbidden love," Lionel said. "Isn't it tragic? But I'll warn you to stay away from her. I want to talk to you."

Rafe froze and let his hands drop back to his sides. He assessed his options and found that most of them sucked. "Isn't that why I'm here? To talk to the council?"

"The council be damned. You're here to talk to *me*."

And that was news. Rafe had, perhaps naively, believed that being invited—well, maybe *summoned* was a better word, now that he recalled the letter—to appear before the Witches' Council meant appearing before the Witches' Council. "All right. About what did you wish to speak?"

"Don't play dumb, Mr. De Santos. It doesn't suit you." Lionel watched him with cold pale blue eyes that looked nothing like his granddaughter's. "We're here to talk about the Accord. It's always been about the Accord."

Rafe shifted, eyes watching Menzies warily. "Tess seemed to think that our opinions about the Accord aren't that different. We both seek to preserve it until we can find the time that best suits revealing ourselves to the human world."

Lionel laughed. "Don't assume you know my goals, boy. I've been working to set my plans in motion for longer than you've been alive. I certainly don't intend to let you derail them now."

"Is this the part where you share your nefarious schemes, while the conveyor belt carries me closer to the spinning saw blades?" Rafe glanced behind Menzies to where Tess lay silently on the floor. God, she looked still. And pale. He bit back a curse.

"You watch too many movies, boy. I'm not planning to kill you. At least, I only plan to kill you as a last resort."

"If you don't plan to kill me, why did you nearly take off my head a few minutes ago?"

"Purely accidental, I assure you. I was aiming for my granddaughter. I'm afraid I allowed emotion to get the better of me again in the first instant after I saw her. I had loosed the energy before I remembered that she's worth more to me alive. At least for the next few minutes."

Again?

Rafe felt sickness and rage boil up in his stomach.

"You were behind that attack," he said, staring at the insane old man before him. "You hired someone to try to kill your own grandchild. Why, if she's worth so much to you?"

"Another momentary lapse," Lionel dismissed. "I'm afraid that when I first learned the little fool had given herself to you, her lack of loyalty made me quite furious. I acted without thinking when I hired that thug. I thought better of it soon enough, but aborting those kinds of actions is just so difficult sometimes. Once I learned that she had survived, and I saw her influence on you firsthand, I knew she might prove useful to me until I had secured your cooperation. Even if the very sight of her makes me sick."

In that moment, Rafe knew he would kill this man, if only because Tess didn't deserve an unfeeling monster for a relative. She deserved better.

"Now," Lionel continued, "ignore the girl for a moment. First, I'm going to tell you why you need to help me make sure the Accord fails here and now."

"Fails?" Rafe jerked back, stunned. "But why would you want the Accord to fail? And why now? Another two or three years and such measures will become obsolete on their own. All you need to do is be patient."

"I've been patient for forty years. I have no more time for patience!"

"Then what do you have time for?" He could feel his own impatience rising, impatience and rage: the frustration at being unable to get to Tess and the rage at the man who had hurt her. "Aside from attacking the people who trusted you."

"They are expendable. And if my granddaughter had been half the witch I had hoped for, she never would have ended up this way. A real witch has the ability to protect herself." He glanced down at her still form, lip curling in a sneer. "It makes me wonder if her mother was quite honest with my dear son, Geoffrey."

Rafe ignored the insult to Tess and reconsidered his options. They all sucked. Until he could get to Tess to protect her, he didn't feel comfortable ripping out Menzies's throat. Not that the image didn't beckon to him like a siren's call, but he wouldn't risk Tess's safety. Not even for that. He couldn't shift while Tess was vulnerable and unarmed and alone, and shifting was about the only thing he could do. A frontal assault would be a really dumb idea.

Of course, it might be his only idea . . .

"Don't look so glum, De Santos." That cold voice

snapped Rafe back to attention and frustration. "I'm willing to refrain from injuring her, and you. You just need to agree to cooperate."

"With what?"

"Pay attention," Lionel snapped. "With dismantling the Accord. As I just said."

"But you still haven't said why."

Lionel stepped forward, his tall frame casting a long, disfigured shadow as he passed under the single, bare lightbulb in the small cluttered storeroom. "Because now is the last chance I have. We're nearing the end of our ability to remain concealed. You said it yourself. Soon, vermin like you and the damned werewolves will be able to walk among human society. And witches—the true heirs to the world—will be viewed as nothing more than another kind of freak. We'll be lumped in with you degenerates. If we're going to act to seize our power, the moment is now. If we strike now and reveal everything to the public immediately, I can control the situation. I can make sure the masses see the distinction between witch and Other. We will become their allies in the struggle against the rise of the unnatural creatures—"

"Holy shit," Rafe breathed. "You are not just crazy, you are absolutely, certifiably insane."

Cut off from his vitriolic rant, Lionel narrowed his eyes. "Insult me all you like. It does nothing to change my plans. I don't require that you assist me willingly."

The witch stood almost directly under the light

now, and the angle cast his face with strange planes and angles. Rafe saw the contrast between dark and light and tensed. Lionel raised his arm, pointing his fingers at Rafe's chest.

"I am one of the finest witches of my age. I can *make* you cooperate."

Rafe paused, weighing the risk of one rash act.

"Do you think I'm hesitant to bespell you, De Santos?" Lionel's voice became louder and more strident. "I am not, you know. I'll do whatever I need to, no hesitation at all."

Hesitation.

Rafe remembered Tess's words and stopped hesitating. He leapt forward. Straight at the lightbulb above the old man's head.

Tess woke to the sound of glass breaking and opened her eyes to see not much more than she could see with them closed. The room around her was pitch dark.

She started to sit up, hoping it would help her get her bearings, but ended up diving right back to the floor, rolling out of the way as two large forms collided in the spot where she had just been sitting. She heard a curse and the growling scream of a big cat and added a curse of her own. Just as soon as she got out of the way.

Stopping when she felt a stack of folding chairs at her back, Tess frantically tried to get her eyes to adjust to the darkness. Her grandfather would have made some comment about how if she were a better witch, she'd be able to cast a spell and get some light, but he was otherwise occupied.

Trying to keep a three-hundred-odd-pound jaguar from feasting on his intestines.

She could hear the sounds of the struggle, but it was quieter than she expected. This was the closest she'd ever gotten to an actual physical fight, and she'd always pictured them being louder, with lots of screaming and shouting and bellowing and the roar of the crowd. Instead, all she heard were grunts and harsh breathing and the sound of flesh and bone making impact. And since the crowd consisted of her, and the last thing she felt like doing was cheering, the scuff of bodies against the concrete floor provided the only accompaniment.

Her eyes followed the sounds and finally picked up a flicker of golden light in the blackness. Rafe's eyes. They glowed with a predatory fury as he wrestled across the floor with her grandfather. Thankfully he was managing to keep Lionel's arms occupied and too busy to cast, or things would have been even more difficult for him. As it was, fighting Lionel Menzies wasn't like fighting an ordinary seventy-five-year-old man. Her grandfather had the strength of magic, and had probably cast some sort of protective spell on himself before coming after them. Tess would have. If she could have.

Damn it, but she felt useless. Here she was cowering up against a row of metal auditorium chairs while the man she'd fallen in love with—damn it again—

tried to save their lives. Couldn't she at least do something?

Damn it a third time, but why couldn't she have been born with some real talent instead of this stupid, useless, no-good, insignificant, nuisance making—

She broke off and stepped to the side just seconds before her grandfather managed to pull away and stagger back against the spot where she'd just been standing. Operating on the strange autopilot of her mini talent, she grabbed a folding chair and lifted it over her head. She was waiting when her grandfather raised his hands and pointed toward Rafe's glowing eyes.

He opened his mouth to sneer. "Now, De Santos," Lionel shouted, "you'll—"

The metal chair smacking down across the back of his head kept him from finishing his sentiment.

"Shut up, Granddad."

It might have been a more dramatic moment if she hadn't followed him to the floor.

Thankfully, she wasn't out long. Probably only a couple of seconds. She came to, feeling the warm, rough scrape of a Feline tongue against her cheek.

"Um, if I needed to exfoliate," she said, eyes still closed, "you could have just said something."

The rumble of his amused purr vibrated right down to her toes, which she flexed experimentally. At least they still worked. Now if only she could get them on the floor under her, she'd be cooking with gas.

She was about to brace her hands on the floor and try it when the door to the storage room swung open and light flooded in from the hall. Followed by a very amused male voice.

"Rafe, Rafe, Rafe. How many times do I have to tell you not to play with your dinner?"

Twenty-two

"Your grandfather tried to kill you."

"I'm trying to focus on the possibility that he only intended to maim me."

Missy collapsed into the sofa cushions beside Tess and shook her head, her brown eyes wide. "But . . . I mean, your *grandfather*."

"Well, it's not like we were close. And I really don't think he knew what he was doing. I think he'd gone a few steps off the sanity trail."

"How do you sound so calm?"

"I'm not dead."

"And where's your grandfather now?"

Tess sighed and rubbed the back of her neck. "Safely out of Rafe's reach. After Graham showed up with the cavalry, we found out there was no council meeting tonight, so we had to take him to the home of one of the council members. He can be watched there until they can have a formal vote on how to handle him. He'll be taken care of, but he won't be getting into any more trouble."

Missy leaned over and hugged her. "I am so sorry, Tess. Is there anything I can do for you?"

"Thanks, but I'm fine." She laughed and sagged back against the sofa cushions. "Actually, it seems almost anti-climactic, until I remember there was no climax to anti. I mean, no one had any idea what was going on until it happened. It was weird. It was like he just snapped. But somehow I still feel like there's something left unresolved."

Missy cleared her throat. "Well, there is the little matter of the curse."

Tess leveled her with a cold stare. "Do you even want me to get started with how not in the mood for that I really am?"

"I don't think that matters much. It seems to be in a heck of a mood for you."

"What are you talking about? Have the preggo triplets come by for another visit? Or maybe my friend Anisia stopped by to yell at me some more."

"I don't know anyone named Anisia, but the triplets have become septuplets."

Tess blinked. "They've what?"

Missy nodded. "Seven. Four more of them crawled out of my woodwork this afternoon. That makes seven new Feline pregnancies in the week since Rafe met you."

"Which is still so not my problem."

Tess ignored the stirring of unease.

"Yes, it so is, actually. Until you came along, there were no Feline pregnancies in Manhattan this year. Zilch. Nada. Not a one. Yet one week after you, a witch, start boinking Rafe, the local Felix, no fewer than seven new women show up to report their pregnancies to the said Felix. Can you think of a single other logical explanation?"

"Fertility clinics."

Missy threw up her hands, "Tess, I swear—"

"Don't, okay?" Tess jumped up from the sofa and glared at her new friend. "Don't swear. Don't swear, don't vow, don't promise—don't frickin' *tell* me. I don't wanna know, do you hear me? This is a Feline thing. An Others thing. Shit, it could be an alien abduction thing for all I know, and that's just it. It's none of my business. If you want to know what's going on, go ask Rafe. Or better yet, present him with the evidence, and then ask him what he thinks. I'm going home."

"I already did."

Tess looked up from using her wrap to cover up the sweatshirt and yoga pants she'd borrowed from Missy. Her unsexy dress had been ruined in the ruckus. "What?"

"I already sent Fawn and the others in to see Rafe. While you were changing. In fact, they should have found him by now." Missy looked toward the doors of the living room. "I can't think what's keeping—"

"TESS!"

Missy smiled. "Ah. I think they found him."

"TESS!"

"Missy, one day I'm going to make you—"

"TESS!"

"—pay for this. Don't you—"

"TESS!"

"—realize—"

"TEEEESSSSSSSSSSSSSSSSSSS!"

Missy raised an eyebrow. "Did that sound closer to you?"

"—what he'll be like?"

The door to Graham's library, where they had been sitting, slammed open and Rafe loomed in the entrance, chest heaving, eyes glowing, hands clenched into fists at his sides. "Tessa Bryony Menzies."

"Yes," Missy said, grinning over Rafe's shoulder at Graham. "I do believe that last one was louder, wasn't it?"

"I think it was, yes. But I'm a bad judge. I think he permanently deafened me. But at least he didn't wake Roark."

The couple stood there and grinned at each other until Tess had to restrain herself from slapping the both of them. She could only watch them from the corner of one eye, anyway. The other one was trained warily on Rafe.

"I think you two need to leave," the Felix growled, never taking his eyes off Tess's face. She wondered if he could see her swallow convulsively. "I want to talk to Tess. Alone."

The menace in that statement made Tess dig in her heels. "That's ridiculous. We're in their house. They don't need to leave. Besides, what do we need to talk about? The stuff with my grandfather is resolved, and the rest of the council said they'd be happy to talk

with you at their next meeting. Everything is resolved."

He half roared. It made him sound like an
irritated . . . well . . . jaguar. "Fine. You do not wish
for privacy? You will not have it. Now tell me why
you never mentioned you were pregnant?"

Missy blinked and sidled around Tess and toward
her husband.

"Right. And on that note . . ." The Luna pushed
against Graham's chest to force him out of the room
and away from the door. "I believe that's our cue to
leave these crazy kids to themselves."

Graham let her tug him down the hall, but before
the door closed behind him, he turned to look over
his shoulder and laughed.

"The carpet in there is not too uncomfortable," he
offered helpfully, "but I recommend you try the sofa
if you're allergic to wool."

Missy dragged him away, scolding as she went.

Tess considered running and hiding behind them,
but it wasn't polite to cause the deaths of one's hosts
in their own home. Still, she couldn't keep her gaze
from sliding longingly toward the door.

"Tess!" Rafe stalked closer to her, looking almost
more like a cat than when he was a cat. Something
about that loose, deliberate way he moved. "Why the
hell didn't you tell me?"

"Tell you what?" She stared at the center of
that loose-hipped stride and forgot about paying
attention.

"Tess . . ." His growl rumbled a warning. "Why did you not tell me you are pregnant?"

That made her gaze snap back to his face. "Not you, too."

"Not me, too, what?"

"You're not going to go on about curses and destiny and me getting seven women pregnant, are you? Because that's, like, all Missy can talk about these days."

"Stop!" He shouted it loud enough to make Tess jump. "Stop trying to distract me and answer the damned question. Why didn't you tell me?"

"Because I'm not."

He opened his mouth to pour out another tirade, but stopped short in surprise. "What did you say?"

"I said I'm not pregnant." She pushed herself up from the sofa and glared at him. "I keep telling people that, and they keep not believing it, but I'm here to tell you that it's true. I. Am. Not. Pregnant."

"Are you certain?"

If Tess had been holding a brick right then, she'd have thrown it at Rafe's head with no hesitation. And a great deal of satisfaction.

"What is it with you people? Yes! I am positive I am not pregnant. Are you happy? Or do you have a rabbit you want me to kill to prove my point?"

His eyes narrowed. "How about you just let me check?"

He was on her before she could tell him what she thought he could go check. He caught her in his arms and tumbled her to the floor, twisting in midair to land on his back and cushion her fall with his body.

"This is all very helpful of you, and I appreciate your offer," she bit out, already squirming to get away and struggling to ignore the way his slightest touch always made her crazy. "But get your hands the hell off me!"

"Not yet." He yanked aside the collar of her sweatshirt and buried his nose against her skin. "Checking."

He inhaled deeply.

Tess cursed and began to struggle. She felt the way her stomach turned over at his slightest touch and knew she needed to get away from him. Touching him turned her willpower into something out of *Mission: Impossible*—it self-destructed after fifteen seconds.

"Hands off, you furry bastard!"

He moved to the hollow of her throat, sniffed again. This time, his tongue darted out to taste her skin. She fought harder.

"I mean it! Get away, you lecherous lycanthrope!"

His teeth closed gently on her throat, and her womb contracted.

"Stop that!"

He didn't stop that. Instead, he brushed aside the tail of her sweatshirt and slipped his hand inside her waistband, fingers gliding across her stomach and burrowing toward her already damp center. Damn him. She whimpered and tilted her hips forward. She felt his fingers dip between her slick folds and find her

entrance. They slid deep, pumped twice, just enough
to get her hips twitching, then pulled away. She suddenly realized she'd stopped struggling to get away.
She was just about to kick him in the shins when he
raised his fingers before him and inhaled. Then he
frowned and licked them, savoring them like a spoon
coated in cake mix.

He sucked the sheen of moisture off his fingers
and purred with pleasure. Then she saw his eyes narrow and he glared back down at her. "You're not
pregnant."

"Argh!" She felt her eyes roll back in her head
and hoped it wouldn't start spinning around while
she spat pea soup. "What the hell have I been trying
to tell you? The same thing I told Missy when she
wouldn't believe me, either! Well, to hell with all of
you! I don't need this shit!"

It would have made a great exit line, except that
Rafe wasn't about to let her exit. When her squirming became almost violent, he simply flipped them
over and pinned her to the floor, making sure to settle between her legs where she couldn't effectively
kick him.

The sneaky bastard.

"Calm down." He said this while he had her hands
pinned to the floor beside her head and his erection
nudged against the flimsy material of her yoga pants.
"Do not be so upset. I was merely surprised. I thought
you had to be pregnant."

"Everybody seems to think I'm pregnant. Bad luck

for all of you." She tried bucking him off, but realized that was a very bad idea when all it did was slide his erection against her already aroused core. She went very still and contented herself with glaring at him. "But I'm not apologizing for taking care of things when you were so hot to trot you didn't even mention the word *latex*."

He reared and those amber Feline eyes glared down at her. "What do you mean you *took care of things*?"

"I mean I took care of things," she snapped, not liking the way his eyes narrowed at her words. "Just because you're irresponsible with sex doesn't mean I intend to be. For God's sake, if I hadn't called Missy in a panic at two in the morning, I'd still be worrying about STDs. You never even bothered to tell me that shifters don't get them."

"You thought I might have infected you?" He was a picture of wounded dignity, but Tess saw his gaze soften. "I would never take a chance with your health, sweet Tess. Don't you realize that?"

"But you did. You took a chance on getting me pregnant, which I had to take care of, and then you act like I'm some kind of villain when I tell you I did the responsible thing."

Oh, shit. His eyes went all narrow and glaring again. "So you did do something to cancel my seed, then. Tess—"

"Oh, give me a break. What the hell kind of phrasing is that? *Cancel your seed?*" She snorted. "It's not like I had an abortion, and if I had, it would have been totally my decision. For God's sake, we had sex for the first time less than two weeks ago. We never talked about pregnancy or kids or even whether we might still be dating by the end of the month."

Rafe looked less than impressed by her logic.

She tried to reason with him, still holding on to the naive hope that he was in the mood to be reasonable. "All I did was make sure that if one of your marauding little sperm happened to breach my defenses, that he'd quickly be shown the door. That's it. It's the responsible thing to do when two adults who should have known better didn't talk about protection before they got down and dirty."

"We will discuss responsibility later," he said, looming over her like a personal black cloud. "Right now I wish to discuss what you used to *show my marauders the door.* Explain."

She sighed and glared right back at him. "Wild carrot seed. I took a tincture every morning after we . . . had sex." She found herself looking away, and realized she'd wanted to say *after we made love,* but she didn't think one person could make love. That was the kind of thing that took two. "It makes the lining of the uterus too slippery for an egg to attach. So, no pregnancy."

He hissed in displeasure. "And you did not think to discuss this with me? You did not think I had a right to be a party to this decision?"

She uttered a strangled scream. "What decision? Rafe, there was no decision. All that happened was me realizing I'd done the stupidest thing in my life and had unprotected sex with a man I'd just met. I realized that, and I took steps to make sure I wouldn't end up paying for it for the next eighteen years. That is not something you needed to be involved in. If you wanted the right to voice an opinion, you should have voiced one before you decided it was okay to come inside me."

He growled, sputtered and growled again. "That's all well and good for the first time, but what about after that? It never occurred to you to discuss it with me?"

"Yeah, about as much as it occurred to you to discuss it with me. I didn't hear you asking if I was on the pill, and you sure as hell never mentioned condoms, so don't try to lay this on my shoulders, Simba. You've got just as much obligation to think these things through as I have."

"I have obligations you haven't even considered," he snarled. "I have an obligation not to let my race die out. And that brings me neatly back to the topic at hand. If you are not pregnant, would you care to tell me why the seven women who just paid me a visit *are*?"

She set her jaw and met his glower with one of her own. It was either glower at him or let him see how much it hurt that he never considered the idea that she might be his mate. "Not my area of expertise, buddy. It's your species and your curse. Figure it out for your damned self."

"That is not an acceptable answer, sweet Tess." His eyes did that glinty thing and took on the distinct glow of mischief. "You have clearly become involved in my curse, or we would not be having this conversation. There have not been seven Feline pregnancies in Manhattan in any given six months since before I was born, yet now I see that many in one week. And the only explanation I can think of centers on you. I find that to be very interesting."

"I find it to be a pain in the ass. That seems to be all anyone can talk to me about. Apparently, that's why all your Other friends like me—not because of my charming smile and gift for witty repartee, but because if you knock me up, your cousins can all do the same with the women they're boinking."

He raised an eyebrow, amusement ghosting across his features. "Boinking?"

Tess felt herself blush. "You know what I mean. It's hardly flattering to know the rest of the world sees me as your saving womb, or something. Especially since that's not even one of the terms of your damned curse."

"And you know the terms, do you? Would you care to refresh my memory?"

"Shouldn't you know it by heart? Isn't that sort of your job?"

He leaned down until his lips brushed hers as he spoke. "Humor me."

"Fine." The self-control she exerted to stop herself from licking his lips should have qualified her for some sort of medal. A Purple Nipple, or something. "From what Missy told me, since you never bothered to, one of your tomcatting ancestors made the dumb move of trifling with the heart of a witch and needed to be taught a lesson."

"Tess . . ."

His warning rumble probably had something to do with her editorial comments, but she didn't particularly care.

"Since the witch was suffering from loving a man who didn't love her enough to stay faithful to her, kittens or no kittens, she cursed him. She said that from then on, no spotted Feline would have an easy time getting the kittens her lover wanted so desperately. Until a spotted Felix found a witch mate and stayed faithful for a year and a day, there would be fewer and fewer children born to the spotted cats. That's what Missy told me, and it looks like that's just the problem you have now, isn't it?"

He purred, his mouth curving into a smirk. "Not anymore."

Tess rolled her eyes. "You don't honestly still believe that I have anything to do with those women getting pregnant, do you?"

She knew she was in trouble the moment she

said that. Because by this point, it sounded normal to her.

"Let's consider it logically for just a moment, shall we? The curse states that in order for the curse to be lifted, a Felix—which could conceivably be you—would have to mate with a witch—and I will concede that I qualify—and remain faithful to her for at least a year and a day. Well, I can tell you right now, Pete Puma, that two out of three does not cut it when it comes to lifting curses!"

His smirk shifted into a grin, wide and pleased and toothy. "You truly do not understand, do you?"

"Understand what?"

That's when he laughed. Laughed! As if he didn't have her pinned to the floor, and she weren't mad enough at him to chew through his hide.

"For a witch, you certainly seem to lack a basic understanding of magic."

"What do you mean by that? Do you think you're some sort of expert?"

"Not at all, but I believe I see what has happened, and I am surprised that you do not."

"Do you work at pissing me off, or is this a God-given talent?"

He shifted her wrists to one hand and used the other to sneak beneath the hem of her sweatshirt again. When she bucked against him and tried to wriggle out of his grasp, he had the nerve to purr with pleasure and angle his hips to hers so that every time she moved, she stroked herself along the ridge of his erection.

"What do you consider to be the basis of all magic?" he asked.

She gargled in frustration. "Don't even tell me you're going to lecture me on spellcraft now. Listen, Sylvester, I've heard all this from my grandfather, and he went insane. I don't need to hear the Magic One-Oh-One speech from you, too!"

He leaned down and nibbled at her neck, his hand gliding up to close, rough and warm, around her breast. "Just answer the question, sweet Tess."

"Will!" She bit it out from between her clenched teeth. What she wouldn't have given just then for the will to keep her nipple from beading eagerly at the first brush of his fingers.

"Very good." He shifted to her throat and licked the hollow there. "And what is it called when you exercise will in order to cause a desired outcome?"

She felt his fingers close around her nipple and pinch, and she couldn't keep her hips from rolling invitingly against his. She felt her folds parting beneath the soft cloth of her yoga pants and his erection nestled against her center as if making itself at home. She moaned.

"In—intent."

"Very good, Tess." He purred it against her throat while he pressed his pelvis into hers, grinding against her and making them both shudder. "Having discussed the topic of magic more than once with my Fae friends, I had been laboring under the impression that the key to spells—and therefore, one assumes, to curses—is to have a clear intent."

Suddenly impatient, Rafe lifted his torso from hers and stripped off her sweatshirt, leaving it tangled around the wrists he still gripped in one hand. Then he leaned close to her, pressing skin to skin, and sighed at the feeling.

Well, he sighed. She moaned. Damn it.

Then he eased down, his hand slipping beneath her waistband and his teeth tugging her bra out of the way, leaving the cup bunched beneath her breast. He lapped once at her nipple and she shuddered.

"So if intent is the key to a curse, my sweet Tess . . ."

God, is he still talking?

". . . what do you suppose was the intent of the witch when she cast her curse?"

He punctuated his question by closing his teeth around her nipple and nibbling. She almost came right then and there.

"Stop dicking around and just tell me what you're talking about!"

She might have screamed it, but she didn't care. Despite the fact that she was lying half naked on the carpet in the middle of the library of a couple she'd met less than two weeks ago.

He laughed and lifted his head, abandoning her breast but plunging his fingers between her legs to tease her soft folds. "You really do not know? Tess, Tess, Tess. What am I going to do with you?"

"I don't know," she hissed, "but if you don't do it in the next thirty seconds, I'm going to have to hurt you."

Her threat made him laugh harder. "Oh, we cannot have that."

The phrase *quick as a cat* sprang to her mind as he shifted off her, stripped them both, and tumbled her back to the carpet. He had her hands pinned again before she realized they were free, but this time when she struggled against him, her shifting hips only succeeded in helping to position him at her entrance.

"Rafe." She murmured his name and twisted her body restlessly beneath him. She needed him inside her again. After all her lectures on responsible sex, he once again had her hot enough to worry about it tomorrow. "Please."

"Of course, my sweet Tess." He slid home with one smooth thrust, driving to the hilt inside her, and making her body arch beneath him. "Is that better, sweetheart?"

She heard the amusement in his dark rumbles and set her jaw. "It will be better . . . once you . . . move!"

She tried to set the rhythm herself, but he held her still. He released her hands to grip her hips and hold her in place. He filled her completely, pressing high and hard inside her and keeping her from riding him the way she wanted. She cried out.

"Hush," he soothed, fingers flexing against her

skin. "You will get what you want in just a minute, baby." He paused, his grin flashing. "Then we'll see if you get a baby."

Tess froze.

"A baby?" she repeated carefully.

He flexed his hips, his hardness shifting inside her, making her moan.

"Do you not want to have children?" He watched her warily.

"It's not that," she said, finding it nearly impossible to concentrate while he stayed buried inside her. "I just didn't think . . . that is, you never said *you* wanted to have them. Especially not with me."

His eyes glowed as he leaned down to kiss her. "You're the key to everything," he told her, his raspy voice suddenly tender. "You lifted the curse. How could I not want you, and a child with you?"

She felt the joy and heat drain out of her at once. Suddenly he no longer felt like a welcome part of her finally back in place, but like an invader trying to conquer her body. "Right. The curse. I'd forgotten. It's all about the curse, isn't it? That's all you care about."

"You are wrong." He grabbed her hands again when she raised them to his chest to push him away. He pinned them down next to her head and forced her gaze to meet his. "I have trouble believing that you do not understand this already, but let me explain."

His voice was rough and hard, but his thrusts were gentle as he began rocking his hips against hers. "What you do not seem to see, my sweet, thick-skulled *gatita,* is that the important part of the curse was not the words with which it was spoken, but the intent with which it was cast."

She heard him, but she also felt him, and she damned her body for betraying her by softening around him and welcoming him deep inside her. If he continued, she'd be lost again, and another little piece of her heart would break off, knowing that she loved him and he just wanted to fuck her.

He leaned down to kiss her softly, and she closed her eyes against the glow of his. If she continued to look at him, she would almost be able to convince herself that the light in his eyes was love. She didn't want to lie to herself like that.

"If the intent is everything, sweet Tess, then the witch's intent was not to force a Felix to remain faithful for only a year and a day. She did not care about time limits." He bit her lower lip, then soothed the tiny pain with the rasp of his tongue. "She cared about love."

Tess's eyes flew open and she gazed up at him. Had Rafe De Santos just said the L word?

"The curse was never meant to withstand love." He moved smoothly above her, every shift and flex another kind of caress, a caress accompanied by the words she was finally beginning to understand. "The minute that old witch got her wish, the curse ceased to have meaning. And that happened the minute a Felix fell in love with his own witch."

He nudged deeply inside her and stopped, resting

against the mouth of her womb, so much a part of her that Tess thought she would die if he separated from her for a moment. She stared up at him and felt her heart stop. She knew then what he was going to say. Whether it was her gift or a different kind of power entirely, she couldn't say, but she knew, and she began to smile.

He kissed her softly, sweetly, lovingly, and pulled back to gaze down at her with a tender golden gaze. "It happened the minute I fell in love with you."

Tess felt her heart expand until it threatened to burst. It pressed up into her throat, making it difficult to breathe, and down into her belly, making her stomach turn a happy somersault. She had to wait for the first wave of joy to recede before she could speak. "I love you, too, Rafael."

He smiled at her like sunshine and resumed his strokes, sliding in and out of her with long, lazy thrusts that soothed even as they aroused. She could feel her climax nearing, more like the gentle swell of a deep ocean wave than like the breakers that crashed over her and threatened to drag her under. She had already gone under, and she didn't mind drowning in him.

She stared up into his eyes as they moved together. He released her hands and she wrapped her arms around him, clutching him to her. Her legs curled around his hips to cradle him close to her. And as she stared up into his eyes, again she knew.

She felt the smile curve her mouth, saw his head tilt and his own smile in response.

"What?" he whispered, brushing his mouth over hers in another of those tender, drugging kisses.

"Just a little déjà vu," she murmured, laughing.

He stilled and his gaze sharpened. "About what? What do you see?"

She slid her hands down the length of his back to his ass, where she squeezed playfully.

"All sorts of things," she teased. "But if you come in the next five minutes, you'll get to make your own mark on repopulating the Feline world."

Rafe's eyes widened, his mouth opened, and the joy that flooded his expression made Tess's heart expand once more. "Really?"

"Really." She smiled through the happy sting of tears and lifted her head so she could tug his lower lip between her teeth. Her body clenched tightly around his, and her fingernails scraped teasingly across his ass. "But if you don't make sure I come with you, I'm naming him Hubert."

The baby, born a standard Feline six months later, was perfect, happy and healthy and thoroughly celebrated.

They named him Gabriel.